Secrets

at

Wallisford Hall

By C.G. Oster

Secrets at Wallisford Hall

Chapter 1

London, 1937

Heels clicking in rhythmic percussion, Dory ran along one of the platforms of Victoria Station, foreseeing the gaps between moving people as she made her way out. Gripping her suitcase firmly, she cursed the cool May wind that tugged on her hair and chilled her legs. It was just about summer. Why was it still so cold?

Grabbing the lapels of her coat, she made her way out onto the streets of Westminster. The walk to Euston would take some time and she couldn't afford to miss her train. Aunt Gladys would not be happy if she arrived late. The call she'd received had conveyed clear desperation. Her help was urgently needed at Wallisford Hall.

Green Park and Pall Mall resembled a construction zone ahead of the new king's coronation. Seating and stands were being assembled, and flags hung. People milled, watching the spectacle before the actual procession. Dory didn't have time to watch any of it.

Checking her watch, she winced. It was a rush to make the twelve-thirty train north. Aunt Gladys' face would crumble in disappointment if she didn't come on the expected train, although Dory didn't entirely understand the reason for the rush. Something about being ludicrously short-staffed for a Coronation Ball.

Dodging buses and motor cars, she weaved through Piccadilly and up along Regent Street. Beautiful frocks lined the shop windows. How she wished she could spend some moments perusing the windows, but it wasn't an option. So rarely did she get a chance to spend time in London, and today, it would simply pass by as she ran from one train station to another.

Going to Quainton to help Aunt Gladys would also make her miss the street party they had planned in Swanley. They had been preparing a whole month for it, and then this call had come—Gladys begging her to come. Mother would not hear a word otherwise, so off Dory went first thing this morning, with barely enough time to even consider that she was packing up and moving. This was the first time Dory left home and it was a shame everything was in such a rush. Maybe not a shame. This way, she didn't have to think about what a momentous change this was. She was growing up—officially leaving her childhood home. Dory didn't have time for tears or worry.

There was probably a more direct route to get there from Piccadilly to Euston, but she only knew the main streets, and could ill afford to get lost. Regent Street led all the way up Euston Road, but there wasn't a single blasted underground station she passed along the way that went to Euston.

People were preparing in the streets here as well, a celebratory mood having settled over the whole country— sponges being baked, sausage rolls, drizzle cake. All that work she had put in at home and she wouldn't partake in any of it.

Her heart beating, her heels clacked down the pavement, which became more navigable once she had passed Oxford Street, finally running past the gorgeous, uniform and white houses of Park Crescent. The minutes of her wristwatch kept ticking by. The game was not up, however. There was still time, but not if she dawdled.

The red brick of the University College Hospital came into view and she knew she was getting close—just a little further and across the road. Euston Station.

Running across the pedestrian crossway, she passed an Indian fellow with a turban. It wasn't every day one saw a turban back in Swanley, she thought, heaving her bag which only seemed to grow heavier. By the time she got to the ticket office, she was so winded she could hardly get the words out. "Quainton Station, please."

"One pound, five shillings," the man said behind the brass bars of the ticket office, a small, green cap on his head.

"Alright," Dory said, taking out her purse and pulling out a crumpled pound note, and fished for the elusive shilling coins. People were gathering in the line behind her as she finally handed them over. The ticket slid to her and she took it.

Everything was fine. She had a ticket and the train wasn't here yet. Still, it would be coming any moment, and it didn't take long until she heard the steam whistle of an incoming train. The concourse was long and brightly lit from the steel and glass roof over the station. Wasn't it marvelous—such a wonderful structure. It still flabbergasted her how large the London train stations were.

Everything in London was on a much larger scale than anything back in Swanley.

By the time she reached the right platform, the train was there with the post compartment open, where heavy satchels were carried out onto large four-wheeled carts. The postmen were still laboring so there had to be a little time before the train left.

Taking a moment, she stilled and tried to recover her breath. Her hair had to be a mess from all that running, but that couldn't be helped. She was here; she was on time. All the rushing had been worth it. There would be no awkward phone call to her aunt saying she had missed the train.

After the disappointing end to her last employment at the Swanley Insurance Office, she couldn't bear to dishearten her family with yet another failed employment attempt. One simple spill had proved unforgivable, but then it had been tea onto the lap of one of the company executives visiting from London, who had received burns severe enough to require a trip to the hospital. No, that had not ended well. She had been dismissed the next day.

A quick look down her legs, she assured herself that her stockings had survived the ordeal of getting here and she couldn't see any runs. All in all, the day was not turning into a disaster.

The postmen were just about finished, so it was time for her to find her seat. *Car C* her ticket said and as they were lettered in sequence, it wasn't difficult to find the right one. She passed by the fine car with the velvet seats to her second-class car, which had more modest green leather seats and scratched wood panels. The floor had wooden slats along it and she had to watch her heels so she didn't topple.

In her compartment were an elderly couple, the woman in a heavy, dark coat and the man in a beige one. Neither had taken theirs off, obviously feeling the cold on this wintery spring day.

"Some weather we're having," Dory said brightly as she entered.

The woman shuddered. "One gets so tired of winter. It never seems to end."

"I'm Dorothy Sparks," she said after putting her suitcase on the netting above her seat and holding her hand out to the elderly couple. "It seems we will be companions for this journey."

They both shook her hand and she seated herself. "Mr. and Mrs. Albert and Flora Clover. Would you like some tea? The thermos is still warm."

"I would love some. Hadn't a moment to refresh myself running here. I had to rush from Victoria Station. I came from Swanley, you see." Pulling out her compact, Dory checked the harm to her blond hair and lipstick. Nothing outright embarrassing, so Dory snapped the compact shut and let it drop into her handbag.

"Yes, we passed there once," Mr. Clover said. "Nice little town. We drove down to the continent. Didn't stop."

"Never been to the continent. It must have been marvelous."

"Oh yes. Strange food, though," Flora pointed out with a serious expression.

"You can't be heading home if you're on this train. This one is going north. Norwest, actually." There was a moment of concern on the man's face, worried that she had gotten herself onto the wrong train.

"I am going to Quainton. Wallisford Hall. I am to be employed there."

Albert looked mollified. "The Fellingworths live there, I believe."

"Oh, you know them?"

"Well, we know of them," Flora responded. "Not really the type to mix, if you know what I mean, or so I have heard." She poured some tea into a small paper cup and handed it to Dory.

"Good land for hunting," Albert said. "Both forest and parkland."

Flora shoved his arm as if he was being silly. "Fairly certain Dorothy here doesn't care a whit about hunting."

The sentiment seemed to surprise Albert, but he didn't say anything.

Dory finished the cup, being more parched than she'd realized. "My aunt works there as the cook and they are short-staffed at the moment. I've had to drop everything and get on the next train. With the coronation coming up… "

"Oh, the coronation. So lovely. They are a lovely family, stable after all that hoohaa about that woman. What was her name?"

"Mrs. Simpson."

"To give up a kingship for a divorcee, and an American... " Flora drifted off with a look of consternation.

"One cannot account for love," Dory said, who had always thought it was awfully romantic. In truth, she wouldn't have minded an American divorcee for a queen, but others found her marital status objectionable. Or even the fact that she was foreign. And Edward was so handsome and Mrs. Simpson divinely smart in her excellent clothes. They would have made a marvelous king and queen. Maybe it was a little more that they broke rules and traditions that Dory admired so much. But not everyone agreed.

It started raining as they left the outskirts of London, streaks of wetness smeared diagonally across the window, which was fogging with the occupants' warmth. It certainly was a dismal day for being May. Hopefully, the king would have better weather tomorrow.

With a sigh, Dory stared out the window, wondering what she was heading off to. She hadn't had time to get used to the idea that she was leaving home. Technically, she was going to live with her aunt, so it was an intermediary step, perhaps. Remembering her hat still on her head, she pulled the pin out and placed it on the empty seat next to her, checking her hair underneath was still relatively tidy.

Chapter 2

The Quainton train station was a small, simple brick building with a parapet painted white and green. Someone had hung strings of union jacks along the edge of it, which were soaked in the rain that hadn't appeased throughout the journey.

With a loud whistle, the train moved with great, heaving chugs of the engine, the steam billowing. Mr. and Mrs. Clover waved through the still foggy window and Dory waved back. The wind was cold out here, the train station exposed to the flat countryside around them. In fact, at first glance, there didn't appear to be a village, only fields, but she must be facing the wrong direction.

Dory didn't know which way to go. Only one other person had gotten off here and she followed him, hoping he knew where he was going. The station building led through to an entrance leading to a street and she followed her fellow passenger out. A few buildings ran along the street, but she didn't know how close she was to the main street, or if this was the entirety of the village. An old green lorry with a large grill stood waiting, the wipers trying to deter the rain.

"Miss Sparks?" a young man said, popping his head out of the driver's side.

"Yes."

"In you get. Quick, quick."

Dory ran to the passenger side and got into the door being pushed open from the inside. The man took her suitcase and put it behind the seat. It wasn't a large compartment, so she sat close to the man who quickly ground the gears into first. "I'm Larry," he said. "One of the gardeners. Mrs. Moor asked me to come fetch you. You're her niece, I understand."

"That's right."

He seemed to watch her for a moment as he pulled out on the road, the engine whirring. "Welcome to Wallisford Hall."

"Thank you, Larry. That is very kind." They drove out of town and down tight country lanes. Wallisford Hall seemed about ten miles from Quainton. "Much to do in Quainton?" she asked.

"There's a pub. There's a windmill."

"Excellent," she said, barely hiding her disappointment.

"Course, there's a picture theater and shops in Aylesbury. Got just about anything you need there. There's a bus that goes every morning and evening if you like." That did sound promising. "I sometimes go myself on a day off. If you wish to go to the pictures, I'd be happy to take you."

"That is a very generous offer. Not sure what my schedule will be like so can't make any such plans just now." And she certainly wasn't going to be stepping out with some young man a moment after meeting him.

Wallisford Hall was grand, bigger than anything she had ever seen. Brick with great, straight towers at each side and large windows throughout the facade, which looked almost a little Elizabethan. There was a bell at the center and the Hall itself had four stories including the towers. It was the grandest house she had ever seen, let alone been to. She couldn't stop staring as Larry pulled the lorry in by one of the adjoining buildings.

"Wallisford Hall is a working farm, of course," he said. "Extensive lands."

"So I've heard. Parkland and forest," Dory said absently.

"That's right," a pleased Larry said, shutting the lorry door with force. "I'll take you to the kitchen entrance. It goes down to the basement where the kitchen and all the facilities are." He led her around the side of the building to a set of stairs which ended by a glossy black door with glass and a brass handle. This was her new home and her new employment. Heat met her as she walked in.

"Dory," Gladys called, coming out of a room. "You made it." Gladys came forward and enveloped her in an embrace. She smelled like butter and flour, but then Gladys always did.

"Aunt Gladys, it's been ages. Well, since New Years. So this is Wallisford Hall. It is nothing like I imagined."

"Oh? How did you imagine it?"

"Oh, I don't know. Maybe a little more gray and stone."

"Like a castle?"

Dory felt ashamed for a moment. Why would she have assumed that? It seemed ridiculous now.

"Now, let me introduce you to Mrs. Parsons, the housekeeper. She is actually the one employing you. I hope your journey went well."

"Nothing to complain about. Met a lovely couple who plied me with tea." They walked down a hall built with white tile and stucco walls. Everything was bright and clean, much more than she'd expect in a basement. To her surprise, she saw what looked like a policeman in one of the rooms as they passed. How strange.

"Mrs. Parsons," Gladys said once they reached a small room with a desk, making up a kind of office. A woman with faded brown hair looked up, her face lined with age and maybe even disapproval.

"Dory Sparks." Shifting her suitcase to her left hand, Dory held out her right.

"Dorothy," Gladys corrected.

"Miss Sparks. We are so pleased you could come on such short notice. I understand you have little experience."

"Well, I've done my fair share of cleaning and bedmaking."

Mrs. Parsons looked unimpressed. "Being a maid in a fine country house takes more than 'a bit of cleaning.' You will have to have impeccable attention to detail, show the utmost respect and also be unimposing. Do you think you can do that?"

"I believe I can manage."

"Dory performed very well at school. Finished all the way through," Gladys added as if she was trying to sell Dory's potential. Dory hadn't realized she'd come all this way simply for an interview. Surely that could have been managed over the telephone. It would be dreadful if she had to make her way home again—and costly.

"I will keep an eye on you and give you direction," Mrs. Parsons said as she rose from her desk and checked the small watch pinned to the lapel of her jacket like nurses have. "For now, perhaps you best settle in your room and then we'll talk about your duties." The dismissing nod was clear.

"Mrs. Parsons runs most of the staff and duties, except the family and the gardens. Mr. Holmes, the butler, takes charge of those. In fact, you should not engage with either unless, of course, one of the family members specifically asks you for something. Do not speak unless you are spoken to, and also do not look people in the eye as they pass. You stand back and wait for them to pass. Understood?"

"Uh huh." Dory was ashamed to say that she was only half listening. There was so much else to pay attention to. Everything here was new, and she desperately wanted to confirm whether it had been a policeman she'd seen in the servants' area of Wallisford Hall.

They walked past the same door and indeed, there was a blue uniformed man scribbling in a small notebook. His policeman's hat was tucked under his arm as he wrote.

"Is that a policeman?" Dory asked, knowing full well it was.

"Yes, nasty business. There was an incident and they are investigating."

"Oh, that's awful. I hope no one was hurt."

"Killed, actually. Your predecessor, Nora Sands. Poor little pet." The concern was evident on Gladys' face as she distractedly wrung her hands.

"You didn't tell me this job was hazardous."

"Being a maid rarely is, but Nora always seemed to attract trouble. She certainly did in the end." Gladys walked ahead to a staircase, obviously unwilling to speak about this subject further. "I'll take you to your room. Can you manage the suitcase or should I get one of the boys to help you?"

"I can manage," Dory said, making her way up the twisting staircase that spun around and around, taking them high up into the house. Probably the fourth floor, which effectively was five floors up, emerging to what was clearly the servants' quarters.

"You have your own room. Not every house has that. Quite a few require the maids to share. Clara and Mavis, the other two maids also have rooms here. I, however, live downstairs, along with Mr. Holmes and Mrs. Parsons, which is a blessing because I don't think my knees could handle all these stairs. I'm no spring chicken anymore."

"Gladys, you are as young as the day you left home."

"You always were a sweet girl. A bit absent-minded sometimes, but sweet. Now unpack and then return to Mrs. Parsons, who will give you your duties."

"Of course, Aunt," Dory said and placed her suitcase on the small bed, glad to finally be relieved of the burden. Her shoulder ached and so did her feet. Gladys left

Dory to familiarize herself with her new lodgings. The walls had pink paper and there was a small window that could be opened to let in some air. Once summer was here, Dory could well imagine this room could be stifling. Taking off her shoes, she stretched her aching arches, the bare floorboards cool on her sore feet. But the room was clean and there looked to be fresh linen on the bed.

Suddenly, it occurred to her that this could well be that girl's room—the unfortunate one who had been killed. Poor girl. Her effects must have been packed up and sent off to her family. Although the fact that there was a policeman downstairs investigating suggested that there must have been more to this than a simple accident. Gladys hadn't mentioned any of this on the phone, but it was obviously the reason they suddenly needed a new maid. Poor girl.

Chapter 3

The reason for the rush in getting a new maid was made clear. There was to be a ball for the coronation and house guests remaining for a few days after. The next morning was a rush of activity. Seemingly all the bedrooms in the house needing airing and dusting, and clean linen put on every bed. Dory didn't have a moment to herself from when she woke at dawn. She missed entirely the actual coronation—too much to do to sit by the wireless and listen to what was happening at Westminster Abbey.

Not knowing where things were was her biggest headache and she often had to run and find one of the other maids to tell her where to find soaps, towels, or cleaning products. By the time she was done with her pressing duties, her hands were red and streaked with black from the coal and wood she'd brought up after everything else was done.

"The family will be arriving soon," Mrs. Parsons said, appearing on the family floor to inspect their work, seemingly going over every detail. She corrected a few corners of the bed and then sighed. "It will do. Take yourself downstairs to help Mr. Holmes prepare for supper."

Behind the closed door of the large and fine dining room, they polished and laid out the table with fine china and silver for supper.

"Traffic was hell," a man said outside. His accent had that bored nasal quality of someone who likely lived in this house, a breed Dory knew little about. Mr. Holmes walked out to greet whoever it was and Dory had the chance to briefly see a young man with wheat blond hair. Handsome and dressed in a finely tailored suit. "Is Mother back yet?"

"Not as of yet," Mr. Holmes responded.

"Good. I have a smashing headache. I think I will take a kip before the festivities start."

The door closed and Dory could only hear mumbling.

"Vivian Fellingworth," Clara said quietly. "The youngest son. Trouble since the day he was born, that one."

"How many children are there?" If he was the youngest, then there were naturally other children. By the look of him, he was well into his twenties, so there weren't any actual children in the house.

"Three, two boys, Cedric and Vivian, and then Livinia. Vivian and Livinia are twins, but Vivian is still seen as the youngest."

"Right."

"Then there is, of course, Lord and Lady Wallisford. They are all coming back from the coronation. They were there in Westminster Abbey, I understand. And the guests." Clara rambled off names Dory didn't know, all sounding very aristocratic. "They are staying, but heaps more are coming for the ball tomorrow night."

"I've never actually seen a ball."

"Well, you won't be seeing this one either," Clara said tartly. "You're here to work, not daydream about balls."

That was a rather unjust accusation, Dory felt. She'd only mentioned she'd never seen a ball. It was a far leap to assume she would be daydreaming about it. "And what of Nora?"

"What of her?" Clara said, her mouth going tight.

"No one has told me what happened to her."

Clara's eyes searched around to see if they were observed. "Killed," she said in barely more than a whisper. "Murdered."

Dory gasped, even though she had been expecting something of the sort.

"Stabbed right in the main foyer. They found her at the bottom of the stairs."

"In the family area?"

"Yes. There was blood in a big pool on the floor. Mr. Holmes cleaned it himself after the police came and took her away. Normally, he makes us clean, but I think he felt it would be too horrible for us. Too right there."

"That is kind, I suppose."

"But what was she doing there? She could have been cleaning and polishing, I suppose, but Mrs. Parsons hadn't given her a specific task to. From what the police said, she was… died in the afternoon. She wasn't far from the main door. Anyone could have come in and… " She drifted off with a worried look on her face. "Anyone. Hopefully, they're long gone by now. I'm scared of going outside, I don't mind saying."

"There are policemen here," Dory pointed out. "I'm sure no one would slip past their notice."

"Of course," Clara nodded. "I think we're done here. We should go downstairs. Cook will need some help."

Dory hadn't seen Gladys all day, so it would be nice to see her. Unfortunately, it wasn't quite time to put their feet up because they were required to help Mr. Holmes serve supper.

The calm silence of the family floor gave away to the more turbulent environment downstairs. Clara walked away to do something and Dory thought she'd go find Gladys, maybe even grab something to eat in the process. She was famished and her supper wouldn't be until after the family had dined, from what she understood.

"And who are you?" a voice said and Dory turned to see a man with brown hair and brown eyes, a handsome, chiseled face. By the look of him, he was not a servant, certainly not a gardener. He wore a coat and a suit underneath. Black shoes, quite worn.

"Dory Sparks. Who are you?" He wasn't the uniformed man she had seen here the day before, but she would bet her shirt that this was a policeman of some variety, probably the one responsible for investigating this case. He had that look about him as if he'd seen too much of humanity.

His eyebrows rose at her directness. "Detective Inspector Ridley. Where do you fit into the scheme of things?"

"I am the replacement that arrived today."

"So, you do not know Miss Sands."

"No, I never met her. Never heard of her before today."

The detective watched her for a moment as if to see if he could spot a lie. Dory crossed her arms and he waved her away. He was a bit rude, she thought, waving her away like some naughty child. She threw a look back at him as she walked. His back was to her and he didn't look her way. Broad shoulders and a straight back. By the look of him, a man who spent most of his days on his feet.

"I just got interrogated by that man out there," Dory said as she reached Gladys in the kitchen, who was spooning broth along a fish poacher. "I'm sure he suspected I was lying. Suspicious lot, aren't they?"

"Comes with the job, I think. Not much good if they can't spot a liar. How are you?"

"I'm knackered and the day isn't even over yet."

"It's usually much calmer than this, but when they wish to entertain, the workload triples. It was why we so desperately needed you to come."

"I understand. Got anything I can eat?"

"Cut yourself a slice of bread over there," Gladys said and Dory walked over to cut herself a slice before spreading butter over it. It was heavenly, or maybe she was simply very hungry.

"Clara, the other maid, thinks someone came into the house and murdered that girl," Dory said between bites.

Replacing the lid on the poacher, Gladys visibly shuddered.

"It's never simply madmen running around the countryside murdering people, is it, though?" Dory continued when Gladys didn't respond.

"What are you saying? Can't be anyone here. Everyone loved Nora."

That wasn't exactly what Gladys had alluded to the day before when she'd said Nora attracted trouble. "But you said she was one to—"

"Off you go," Gladys said sharply, just about bundling her out of the room. "Can't you see how busy I am?"

"Sorry," Dory mumbled through her mouthful of bread. Then she found herself out in the corridor again. That man was still there, DI Ridley. He looked over her way again and dismissed her as unimportant. To him, she probably was completely unrelated to his investigation. In truth, she might be the only person who was.

Poor girl. Stabbed. How awful. This man was now here to find out what had really happened to her and to cart away the person responsible. Dory did feel better having him here. Unfortunately, she couldn't bring herself to believe the theory that some stranger had come and randomly murdered someone. It never happened like that, did it? Not really. Someone was responsible and chances were that it was someone she knew. Maybe that was why

DI Ridley was here in the house, questioning everyone. He obviously believed the culprit was here as well. That thought was certainly disturbing.

There wasn't time to dwell on it for much longer as the family and some guests were arriving and Dory had to unpack their belongings. It was strange taking someone else's belongings and putting them away. Dory was assigned to a Miss Alsaze, who had the finest things Dory had ever seen. Nightclothes made of the softest silk and brushes with fur bristles and gilded handles. Golden-cased makeup and the most wonderful clothes and shoes—quite a world away from her own wardrobe. This was more like what Mrs. Simpson wore. Gorgeous things that each cost more than Dory's worldly goods.

Once everything was hung away and placed out, she built a fire in the room before leaving. Now onto the supper. It would be well past ten in the evening before she had her own. She was actually starting to regret losing that job in the Swanley Insurance Office where they got to go home at five-thirty every day. Domestic service seemed to be much more demanding for roughly the same pay. Maybe she should consider secretarial school.

Chapter 4

"The way I hear it, Herr Himmler gathered up the whole of the criminal element and sent them to a workcamp," said a woman in a cream silk dress with ruffles along the shoulders, a cut crystal glass in hand as she sat around the dining table. "One fell swoop. You can't accuse them of not being effective. These people who plague all of society—removed and put to useful work. It is something to be applauded, isn't it? Those Nazis certainly are decisive."

"It remains to be seen what Chamberlin does when he takes over," responded a man with combed black hair.

"Largely, he'll have the same policies as Baldwin. War needs to be avoided and the Germans agree," another man spoke while leaning back from the soup dish before him.

Dory waited so see if anyone wished for more, but all around the table seemed content with their portions. Her hands had shaken as she'd carried the plates over from the serving table, deathly aware that she could not afford to spill a single drop. Mr. Holmes was watching everything she did.

"Yet they are building bombers up in Yorkshire. That can hardly go unnoticed," the woman continued.

"Of course we must hope the Germans will be reasonable, but can we depend on it?"

"He is right, of course. War with Germany would be absolutely disastrous for Britain. If Britain needs to focus on anything, it's paying attention to the colonies—restoring where we must, not off fighting with the Germans. So Hitler claims Austria. He does have a point. There are ancestral claims to be considered. The local populace seems to welcome it."

"Just like we rolled over when the Italians took Abysinnia," said the blond man that Dory had seen arriving earlier that day. "Isn't appeasement simply a case of us preparing for the fact that we have no means of responding when a fascist dictator decides to take what isn't theirs?"

"Vivian," chided an elegant older woman at the end of the table. She was a little older, dressed in a spectacular green dress, the material shining like an emerald. Dory had to assume this was Lady Wallisford, and probably the mother of the blond younger man.

Vivian shrugged and drank deeply of the white wine.

After the soup had been served, Mr. Holmes gave Dory a discreet nod that suggested she take herself down to the kitchen. Laughter chased her as she quietly went through the door, then silence for a moment as she walked down the stairs to the kitchen below that was a hive of activity. Fish was being served with cream on a silver plate, some greenery being placed for decoration.

"Just about ready," Gladys said with pride. It looked mouth-watering and Dory felt her stomach grumble. Gladys was a good cook; Dory could attest to that. "Mind you don't drop that now, girls. There will be hell to pay if you do."

Dory didn't need the reminder. She was nervous enough already. The dish was heavy and it took both her and Clara to carefully carry it up, also ensuring the fish didn't actually slip off the plate when they navigated the stairs.

"Edward is already in France, I understand," the cream silk woman said. "They must be preparing for the marriage."

"I heard it said his royal highness won't be so royal anymore, that by abdicating, he has given up his royal status completely." This was from the other young man, hair a bit darker than the blond one. Dory guessed it was the other son of the family, Cedric, if she recalled right.

"Not sure about that, but over my dead body will I bow to that harlot and call her 'royal highness'," said a man with a severely thin nose. In entirety, the man looked disapproving, and Dory suspected that was both a permanent expression and disposition.

In a way, she found this fascinating, almost like she was observing these people at a zoo. They were completely different, maybe even a different species for all she knew. A drop from her large silver spoon fell on the tablecloth of the side table as she'd started serving and she could just about hear Mr. Holmes wince. As interesting as it was observing these people, she couldn't get careless. She had a job to do. Focusing anew, she refused to look at anything other than what she was doing serving portions of fish onto plates.

Mercifully, supper finished and the dining party moved onto the parlor to continue their evening. Mr. Holmes would take care of their needs now, which left Dory and Clara to clear and wipe down the table. Their own supper was finally in sight and Dory felt hunger bite her insides. With her fingers, she stole a portion of fish, which melted in her mouth. There were some leftovers, so part of her supper might include fish.

A table in the scullery was where everything went. That was the end of Dory's job for the night. The scullery maid would see to the rest. Sitting down in the servants' dining room, Dory put her aching feet up. "What a day." In fact, every muscle in her body ached.

Both Gladys and the scullery maid, Sarah, were putting dishes on the table. Dory supposed she should get up and help, but it felt so nice sitting down and she couldn't bear to put any more pressure on her feet, so she was a little lazy. In exchange for this laziness, she felt considerable guilt, but no one was giving her any particularly nasty looks.

People started streaming in, including Mrs. Parsons, who seated herself at one end of the table. Finally, Mr. Holmes arrived, having seen to the family and guests' drinks for now. He said a quick grace and they all served themselves from the spread in front of them. The food was nothing to scoff at. They ate well. There were steaming potatoes, beans, bread, fish and some kind of braised beef. It all looked spectacular and Dory savored every bite.

"How was your first day, Dory?" Mrs. Parsons asked once the initial enthusiasm for eating subsided.

"I don't mind telling you my feet ache mercilessly. Having come from working in an office, they are not used to being so active."

*

The next day was manic. So many guests were expected for the upcoming ball, they had to air out and dust just about every room in the house. Old linen and towels had to be hung and aired. Mrs. Parsons worried about the hot water, determining they might have to heat water the old-fashioned way if they were in a pinch—boiling it on the fire.

Much needed doing, and Dory had been charged with the last-minute finishing touches, including polishing all fingermarks off the staircase banister. In truth, it was a task she didn't half mind because it didn't include running around. She could even sit down on the stairs for a while as she worked. Her sore feet hadn't gotten much of a reprieve. They would harden up, Gladys assured her—had just had too soft a time of late.

The polish was lovely, actually infused with lavender oil, the scent wafting as she worked the fine leather shammy over the mahogany wood.

"I really must have a word," a man's voice said down below.

"Mr. Ridley," replied the sharp voice of Lady Wallisford.

"DI Ridley," he corrected. There was a hint of annoyance in his voice, although nowhere near as blatant as Lady Wallisford's, who came into view walking with Mrs. Parsons.

"DI Ridley," she said with exasperation, "I have a ball to plan. I cannot run around answering questions about something I know nothing about. For all I know, it was an accident. Who's to say she didn't stab herself falling down the stairs?"

"In the back?" he said dryly.

"It could happen. The silly girl was known for being accident prone. I'm sure she had the unfortunate luck of stabbing herself falling."

"It wasn't an accident," DI Ridley said in return. The assurance in his voice said he knew it wasn't an accident. Dory supposed they could tell on the body whether she fell or not, but stabbing oneself in the back while falling would be absolutely extraordinary.

Lady Wallisford waved her hand as if some insect was annoying her. "This will all have to wait, I'm afraid. I don't have time to deal with it. I can't be expected to do your job for you, DI Ridley. If you are so convinced this wasn't an accident, perhaps you should speak to the people around the district, see if they've seen any strange men around. Mr. Holmes, would you see the detective out."

The butler appeared, looking unsure how to proceed, because one didn't just show detectives from the police out on a whim. Grudgingly, DI Ridley closed his notebook and walked to the door. Lady Wallisford disappeared into the library without a look back. Dory had never seen such rudeness, but perhaps the woman was simply a nervous type who couldn't deal with upsets or commotions.

Needless to say, the expression on DI Ridley's face wasn't one of cheery compliance. Dory felt embarrassed on his behalf. It was unconscionable that he be treated that way. He was only trying to help, after all, to solve a murder, but to Lady Wallisford, that was an insignificant pursuit compared to this ball. Clearly, the lady wasn't one for heartfelt consideration when it came to the staff, or was it something specific to Nora Sands she didn't like? Dory didn't know the woman well enough to tell.

Chapter 5

"Was Nora Sands well liked?" Dory asked as she sat down to breakfast shortly before dawn. Sleep still affecting her, she had trouble keeping her eyes open. Supper had been a late affair and more guests had arrived.

"Of course she was liked," Gladys said, annoyed at the question. "What a thing to ask."

"Well, someone clearly didn't like her."

Gladys grumbled. Mrs. Parsons appeared, looking perfectly put together. In fact, Dory had never seen her anything but perfectly presented. "Miss Dorothy," she said and turned her attention to Dory. What had she done now? Surely, she couldn't have done so very wrong with the polishing, and there had been no notable incidents at supper.

"Yes, Mrs. Parsons," Dory said as brightly as she could muster this time of the morning.

"His lordship's sister is arriving this morning, and she will be staying through the summer without a maid. You will have to tend to any of her needs. Understood?"

"Yes."

"Now, I know you have little experience as a ladies' maid, and you are barely qualified as a general cleaning maid, but we have to make do in these extraordinary circumstances, particularly over this weekend."

"Of course," Dory said, wondering if she should be dreading this.

"I will perhaps have to explain to Dowager Lady Pettifer that you are unfortunately rather inexperienced."

Dory nodded and Mrs. Parsons continued. "We are placing her in the west blue room, and she is arriving shortly, so best you wait there." Mrs. Parsons looked down at the half-eaten bread in Dory's hand. "After you are finished, of course." Turning sharply, she left and Dory looked over at Gladys.

"Lady Pettifer won't bite," Gladys said. "She is the nicest out of the lot of them. Been a while since we've had her here. Usually lives in France. You speak French, don't you?"

"Only the barest."

"I thought your mother had said you'd learnt."

"I tried, but Mother exaggerates if she says I know French."

With a nod, Gladys got up and walked out, making her way toward the kitchen to prepare breakfast for the family and their guests.

*

'Shortly' turned out to be closer to midday and for a couple of hours, Dory helped Mavis put linen in the rooms. Mavis was a proper ladies' maid and tended to Lady Wallisford most of the time. As a result, she did less scrubbing and carrying, except today, when her labor was desperately needed in preparing the guest rooms.

"I told you to wait in the blue room," Mrs. Parsons said, appearing in the hallway.

34

"I was helping Mavis."

"Dowager Lady Pettifer is here and there is no one to tend to her." The rebuke was sharp in Mrs. Parsons voice.

"I'm sorry. I was just trying to help."

"And now you must see to your mistress."

Dory ran down the hall toward the west blue room and quietly knocked on the door. "Come in," she heard from the door and she quietly stepped inside. A woman was sitting at the dressing table, her dark blue hat on the dresser in front of her. Gray hair was neatly clipped into place and light blue eyes surveyed Dory through the mirror. Dory did a bobbing curtsey. "My maid, I take it," she said, her skin was powdered around her rounded chin.

"You can call me Dory."

The woman turned around and looked at Dory properly. "Quite informal, aren't you?"

"I suppose." Had she put a foot wrong already? Perhaps Mrs. Parsons was being too hopeful thinking she could be a ladies' maid.

"In that case, I will call you Dory, just here between you and me." She turned away again. "I'm glad you built me a fire. I do so suffer in the cold English weather."

"I understand you live in France," Dory said, not knowing if she was being too forward. Essentially, she was breaking Mrs. Parsons 'no speaking unless spoken to' rules.

"The south of France, actually. The Cote de Azure. I find the weather there suits me." As far as Dory could tell, there wasn't rebuke in her voice, so the lady didn't seem to mind her speaking. "Where is that other girl, the one I had last time?"

Dory's smile slid from her face, because she guessed it hadn't been Mavis. "Miss Sands had an unfortunate development." As she recalled that was along the lines of what Mrs. Parsons had said when Dory had first arrived, or something to that effect.

"Oh, I am sorry to hear that. Nothing bad, I hope."

This really shouldn't be her position, telling this woman, but it was a direct question. Technically, she needed to respond. "Quite bad."

Lady Pettifer's eyebrows rose as she was waiting for a response. Was there a delicate way of putting this? Dory was searching for one. "It appears she was attacked. Fatally so." The shock was evident on Lady Pettifer's face, and clearly, Lord and Lady Wallisford hadn't felt this was news that needed to be shared with anyone.

"In the village?"

"At the bottom of the stairs," Dory said carefully, vaguely pointing.

The woman gasped, but she remained quiet after that, tending to something on her dressing gown while Dory unpacked her trunk, hanging up the dresses and putting away toiletries. Whenever Dory looked over the woman was distracted. "That is distressing to hear," Lady Pettifer finally said. "I am so sorry for her family."

"Yes," Dory agreed and wondered if Lady Pettifer was more sorry than any of the other family members. "There has been a detective here asking questions."

"And has he found anything?"

"Not that I can tell. Obviously, I'm not in his confidence, but it seems he is asking questions of everyone, although not all are giving him the easiest time of it."

"Is that so?" Again, Dory worried if she'd just said something she shouldn't have.

"Did Mrs. Parsons inform you that I don't have a great deal of experience? I'm the replacement, you see, made on short notice. I am the niece of Mrs. Moor, the cook. I've worked mostly in offices—insurance."

"I see," the woman said with a smile that made her whole face soften.

"So you will forgive me if I do anything wrong, and please tell me if I do."

"And how are you finding working in a country house?"

"I hadn't expected it to be quite so murderous."

The woman chuckled. "No, I dare say not. I suppose they are assuming it was some madman come and randomly murdered the girl."

"It has been mentioned once or twice."

"Murder is rarely some madman. There is typically a reason," Lady Pettifer said.

"That's what I said, but I find people prefer to believe otherwise."

"Which means there is a murderer in our midst. How distressing. We shall have to watch our surroundings." The woman visibly shuddered.

"DI Ridley seems a very competent man. I am sure he will catch the culprit in short order," Dory said, trying to comfort the woman, feeling responsible for being the one to tell her. "Now is there anything you need?"

"Perhaps you could press my gown for tonight while I rest. I will stay in my room for the rest of the afternoon. Return early evening and help me dress."

"Of course," Dory said, taking the gown she had just hung on a hook inside the wardrobe door. Quietly as she could, she left the room, again wondering if she had been much too liberal with her thoughts. Although knowing that she was wondering probably meant yes, she had not acted with the quiet deference she should have. Lady Pettifer had made no indication that she minded.

The supper ahead of the ball was much more informal, more a banquet with trays from which people could choose. Dory had to help, and to clean away plates as needed.

There seemed to be a hundred people there and it was hard to keep up. Long slim gowns in every color milled around, including ostrich feathers and fur collars. Jewelry of the most exquisite tastes was draped around necks and wrists. Women even wore glittering, bejeweled tiaras. Dory caught herself simply watching at times, forgetting the work she was supposed to do in her drab uniform. It was a scene unlike one she had ever seen, one she absolutely didn't belong in. It was hard not to indulge in watching the ball scene in front of her, which every girl who'd ever been told a fairy tale would automatically be drawn to.

Lady Wallisford loved the attention, wearing a gown made of a burnt gold material. Dark feathers embellished the bottom of the skirt. It would be impossible to clean that dress, Dory thought. Lord Wallisford and his sons all wore black tie, impeccably cut garments that were obviously sewn to fit their frames. The best suits money could buy.

The blond one was flirting with a woman— successfully too, by the look of it, while the darker haired one was standing with his father amongst a group of men smoking cigars. Glasses of champagne were handed out by waiters that Dory knew were not part of the staff of the house.

For being a ball, there was actually very little dancing. There were the few couples in tight embrace, moving to the rhythm of the playing band. Somehow Dory had expected more, but obviously, this wasn't that kind of ball. There were going to be fireworks later, though, close to midnight.

There would be little sleep that night and a mountain of work to do in the morning.

Across the large ballroom, Dory saw Lady Pettifer in the gown that Dory had refreshed. She spoke to women similar to her age. The woman must have gone to balls her whole life. Dory couldn't image what it would be like to be invited to a ball like this. Obviously, she'd been asked to the dance hall a time or two, and jewelry and fine gowns besides, it wasn't all that different, was it? Although she wished the young men who asked her out looked as smart in their clothes as the Fellingworth boys did in their tuxedos. That would be the day.

Chapter 6

Dory refused to sleep away most of her day off even if she easily could. It felt so lovely not to drag herself out of bed at the crack of dawn, but equally, she wanted to explore this place she now found herself in. Some of the staff were going to Aylesbury shortly after Sunday service, but Dory was going to stay in Quainton. Yes, Aylesbury was larger and had more amenities, but first, she wanted to see more of Quainton than the train station. She could have lunch in the pub, then walk home from there. It was going to be lovely, she decided.

Quainton might not be large, but for a first time, she was sure there was plenty to explore. It also had a little store from what she understood and she would buy a magazine. Larry the gardener had mentioned a windmill. She'd never actually seen a real one before.

Dragging herself out of bed, she dressed. The air wasn't quite as chilly that morning, so hopefully, it would be a gorgeous spring day. They could use some nice weather after the long winter.

There was a stillness when she reached the basement. The endless little tasks of ironing, carting, polishing and a hundred more had all been put to the side. A light breakfast was served to the family and any remaining guests after the party yesterday. Lady Pettifer hadn't needed assistance this morning, for which Dory was grateful.

Many of the staff were sitting around the dining table in silence as Dory walked in, lost in their own thoughts, or reading the paper like Mr. Holmes. Gladys smiled, finishing off her eggs and kippers, already dressed for going to church. Being a bit late, Dory had to hurry as they were leaving soon.

It turned out that the estate had several vehicles, and the staff squeezed in wherever they could. George, the driver, was taking the family in the large Salmson. Cedric had to sit up with George to make room in the back. By the looks of it, Vivian hadn't made it.

The church was beautiful, old and stone. Dory tucked her hands under her thighs to keep warm when they sat down in the cold pews. Surprisingly, her breath wasn't condensing in front of her. The clear spring day outside hadn't reached inside the church, it seemed. The family sat in the front pew. Dory saw Lord and Lady Wallisford, Cedric and Lady Pettifer. Vivian was still absent. Perhaps he had returned to London, or wherever he dwelled.

It wasn't a long service, and Dory was grateful they didn't have a reverend who wanted to keep them as long as possible, as if their eternal salvation was predicated on sheer stamina. In fact, the reverend was quite handsome. Late twenties, perhaps. He looked kind. In a way, it was a shame because she could never make a true confession to a handsome, young man. It just went against the grain.

And then they were free. Clara and Mavis went with Larry, who made a half-hearted attempt to get her to come to the pictures, but she actually wanted to spend some time on her own. Sometimes she needed that. And on a beautiful day like this, what point was there spending it inside a dark picture theater? Gladys was having lunch with a couple of the ladies from the village, but Dory declined the invitation. She waved them all off as they left, relishing the opportunity to spend some time without their company. That sounded ungenerous, but spending all week with them was enough without keeping them company on her day off as well. Alright, there might be a tinge of guilt at her own reclusive behavior, but that couldn't be helped.

Most of the village was built of the same stone as the church. There had to be a quarry somewhere near that had been used to build the village. Some houses were red brick, looking more like Swanley. It was beautiful and peaceful, quiet on a late Sunday morning. The windmill with its long sails could be seen from anywhere in the village. All in all, it was a lovely village.

A dark thought crept into her mind. If not someone from Wallisford Hall, then someone from this village had murdered Nora Sands. Suddenly, the cheery facades of the village buildings looked more ominous. There could potentially be a secret hiding amongst these houses, something that caused a person to murder a young woman. Was Nora a local girl? Dory didn't know, had never thought to ask.

Feeling the need for a constitutional, Dory made her way to the pub. It was warm and welcoming, a building with a low ceiling and all sorts of interesting knick-knacks nailed along the walls and ceiling beams. Polished wooden tables filled the space and Dory claimed one, ordering a steak and kidney pie.

Farmers stood around the bar, chatting and drinking even at this early hour. As her gaze traveled along, she saw DI Ridley sitting in a corner with a glass of ale in front of him and reading a paper. Dory guessed he lived upstairs for the duration of his stay. No doubt a village like Quainton could not support a full-time detective. He had to be from Aylesbury or even further away—Oxford or even London.

Dory watched him for a moment, his brown hair was neatly combed. There was no ring glinting on his finger, so he wasn't married. Neither had he been in the church that morning, which meant he either didn't attend outside his own parish, or he didn't attend at all. For a moment, she considered walking over there and joining him. No doubt he could answer whether Nora Sands was local or not, but then he might not appreciate discussing the topic on what appeared to be his day off. Did policemen have days off when they worked a case? She had no idea.

Grabbing her seltzer, she picked up her handbag and walked over. "DI Ridley. Dory Sparks. This must be where you keep yourself when you are not intently questioning up at Wallisford Hall."

He looked up for a moment, and stared blankly at her as if trying to place her. "The new staff member."

"That's me," she said, sitting down. "I was wondering if Nora Sands was a local girl."

DI Ridley took a moment to consider her before answering. "No, she was from Banbury up north from here. Norwest to be exact. Why do you ask?"

"I was just curious, I suppose. I have her room now, you see. None of her effects are there, but I can't not be reminded of what happened to her. I suppose the culprit must either be from the Hall or from this village."

"Yes," he said guardedly.

Her steak and kidney pie arrived. "Care if I join you?"

"It appears you already have."

"I take it you have been sent here from London or Oxford."

"London. The Met."

Grabbing the knife and fork, she prepared to demolish the neatly constructed pie. "Must be quite a change for you being in such a small village. In a way, it must make it easier because the suspects are confined in both number and space, where everyone knows everyone. Hard to hide a crime in a small village."

"You would think so," he said dryly. "Are you particularly interested in crime, Miss Sparks?"

"Not really. I suppose, it was a constant issue where I worked at the insurance office. When money is involved, people are more likely to do things out of their character."

"Or show their true character."

The pie was rich with thick, spiced gravy. The peas were fresh, maybe even picked that morning. Dory was pleasantly surprised. "You must be good at judging characters."

"I am fooled sometimes, but not often."

"I am sorry Lady Wallisford was so rude to you. It was unnecessary."

"I doubt she would like you to speak on her behalf."

His brown eyes observed her and she wondered what he thought. He gave little away. "My aunt said that Nora had a way of constantly getting herself into trouble."

"What is that supposed to mean?"

"I don't know. She didn't elaborate."

"Well, thank you for telling me, Miss Sparks."

Dory smiled, glad she could be of help. In short order, her pie was finished and an awkward silence developed. "I suppose I should get going. There are a few things I want to do before I return to the Hall. Can't quite call it home yet. Perhaps that will change in time. The field of domestic service is new to me, so not sure I will ever feel at home in someone else's house, particularly in the room of a girl who was so horribly… dispatched."

DI Ridley didn't say anything, but he nodded to her as she rose from her chair and grabbed her handbag. She felt like she wanted to say something else, but couldn't quite think what. "If you need assistance with anything, I would be happy to help."

"Thank you for the offer. I do have men who are paid to do so, as many as I need, actually."

"Of course," she said, feeling foolish. Blushing slightly, she nodded to him before leaving, the bell over the pub door tinkling as she opened it. She wasn't sure what to make of DI Ridley. A guarded man, without a doubt, but perhaps as a policeman, he had to be. It would hardly work well if he went and spilled all his thoughts and theories.

Interestingly, though, Nora Sands was not a local girl, although she had been at the Hall for a while—long enough to form relationships in the village that could turn sour. Still, enough to murder? Well, the insurance office had taught Dory that murder sometimes required very little incentive.

Chapter 7

The village shop contained a little of everything from household goods, to sewing materials, food and even books. There were magazines and Dory bought herself a copy of the latest Cosmopolitan. She liked the fiction serials in them and was happy to know she could continue the story she had already started. She also bought some caramels in a small, brown paper bag.

The shopkeeper was an older man with an apron. He was curious about her, but didn't ask. Obviously, he would know everyone in the village, and she would be a new face.

"Dory Sparks," she said to introduce herself. "Up at the Hall."

He made an understanding noise and nodded. "Replacing that girl, the one they found?"

"That's me."

"Terrible."

"Yes, it is. Did you know her?"

"Liked Jelly Babies. Came in quite often, almost every Sunday on her way back to the Hall."

"Oh," Dory said and thanked him when he returned her change. So Nora had been in the village almost every weekend, which meant she wasn't going off to Aylesbury with the rest. Informing DI Ridley of this came into her mind, but she guessed he already knew this. Of course he would have asked such people as the general merchant.

The door to the shop rang as well as she walked out to the cobbled main street of Quainton. Produce was stacked in boxes outside the shop and she wondered if she should buy an orange while she was here, but decided not to return into the shop.

A blond man was walking toward her and the shop, wearing a tweed suit with a yellow waistcoat—much fancier than any of the men in the pub. Vivian Fellingworth. So he hadn't left the area, after all, had simply chosen not to attend Sunday service. Or was he returning after a night away? He looked up when noticing she was in the way, his clear blue eyes on her. "You look familiar," he said.

"I serve you supper most nights."

"Ah. The new girl. Sorry, I forgot your name."

"We were never actually introduced. Dory Sparks." She held out her hand, not really knowing what else to do. Was she supposed to curtsy? It seemed terribly awkward doing so here and now, outside of the house where their relationship wasn't quite the same as it was inside the house. Was shaking hands even appropriate? He took her hand in his. It was warm and not quite as soft as she'd imagined.

"If you're returning to the Hall, I can give you a ride in a minute. Just need some tobacco. Hang on a moment." He disappeared into the shop, the bell over the door tinkling again. Dory saw him chatting amiably with the shopkeeper. This man was a natural charmer, Dory realized. But then she had also seen him be contrary to the point of rudeness.

"So, what brings you to Wallisford Hall?" he asked when he emerged again.

"A sudden vacancy."

"Ah, the girl."

"Did you know her?" Dory asked.

"A little. One does get to know the staff over time. It's only natural. Nice girl. Pretty. It's a shame what happened to her. Too young for such a fate."

"What did happen to her?" Dory said as she followed him to his large, white car. If he was offering her a ride back, she was going to take it over a long, sweaty walk back. It would give her more time to do nothing other than read and maybe even put a treatment in her hair, although she was conscious that DI Ridley may be watching them from inside the pub. The idea made her feel uncomfortable, but she wasn't entirely sure why.

"Not sure. I only saw the aftermath. Quite a shock. Not what I had expected waking up that morning."

"So, you were there?"

"You're sounding a little like that policeman who has been skulking around."

Dory blushed. "I'm sorry. I am just interested, I suppose. Someone being murdered isn't the most typical thing, is it? Not what you wish to learn taking on a new position of employment. Surprise, the girl before you was murdered."

"Did no one tell you?"

"No, I learned about it the day I arrived."

"Perhaps they thought you'd run screaming for the woods."

"Maybe someone in their right mind would."

Turning the key, the engine started to rumble. This was a much finer car than the one she had arrived in. The canvas top was down, the insides in red leather. In fact, it was the finest car she had ever seen. "Been out driving?"

For some reason, she didn't seem to be able to treat him with the deference she perhaps should, not out here on a village street. If delivering water to his room, or serving his supper, then yes, but not here. It seemed wrong, and so far, he hadn't kicked her out of his fancy car.

"Drove some of our guests down to London last night."

His not-as-soft-as-expected hand shifted the gear as he pulled out. In fact, he was a little more substantial in form in general, as if he enjoyed sports. That might explain the sun-kissed skin. In fact, all of him appeared to be golden. Looking over as he pulled out, he smiled. Nice, straight teeth. Vivian Fellingworth had been given gifts in the looks department.

"Have you been traveling of late?" she asked.

"What makes you ask?"

"You appear to have seen a bit of sun lately." Or else, he lived in some microcosm where the spring hadn't been a cold, wet affair.

"You really are interrogating me, aren't you? Are you always this curious? You sound just like that detective. Maybe you have missed your calling in life."

Dory blushed again and looked away. "One of my traits, I'm afraid." One her mother had barraged her for endlessly. Perhaps she should try to remain quiet during the rest of this journey.

Vivian pursed his lips. "It's a strange thing being questioned by that man. He seeks to know everything there is to know about you while at the same time not having any real interest at all. Disconcerting, if you're not used to it."

"I only got a passing sense of it as I arrived after the fact; hence, immediately of no interest to him."

Golden man remained silent for a moment. "I hope this business wraps up quickly. It certainly isn't nice having accusations thrown at you."

"Have there been?"

"Well, no, not directly, but the insinuation is there. I suppose it would be with everyone he questions."

The car traveled fast down tight country lanes, at times a little too fast for Dory's comfort. Vivian Fellingworth was very assured with his driving, as if he was an old hand at it. But he couldn't be that old. There wasn't a single line on his face, his skin smooth and tanned.

The wind whipped her hair as they drove. It felt strange sitting next to a person and not saying anything. She'd promised herself she wouldn't ask any more questions. "Do you live at Wallisford Hall permanently?" So much for that intention.

A deep sigh escaped him. "I've just returned from Cambridge. I spend most of my time there. We have a townhouse in London, of course, but I find I get much too distracted in London. Or rather, Father fears I get too distracted."

"Do you?"

A smile spread across his lips and he looked over. "Of course. These last few months, though, Mother insisted I stay in Cambridge every weekend to prepare for my exams so I don't distract myself too much. Didn't like it, because Cambridge can be a bore on the weekends, but it had the desired effect. All exams passed."

"So what do you do now that your studies are finished?" What did the sons of the manor do? Vivian was a second son, so he wasn't set to inherit Wallisford Hall.

"Haven't exactly worked that out yet. What about you, have you had your heart set on domestic service?"

"God, no. I only came because Gladys, my aunt, asked me to. More like demanded. Not sure I'm cut out for it. For one, I tend to ask too many questions. I'm sure you've noticed."

"You'd make a good lackey for that policeman."

"Do you really think so?" she said, probably with more enthusiasm than she should. "That would be awfully exciting, wouldn't it? Although, I suspect one becomes quite jaded with humanity doing such work."

"You think DI Ridley is jaded?"

"I think he's hard to impress."

"Didn't realize you were trying to impress him. Now that is interesting."

How had they gotten on this topic? Things had twisted out of all proportion. "I'm not. I'm just good at asking questions, is all I'm trying to say."

The look on his face showed he wasn't convinced. Wonderful, now Vivian Fellingworth thought she had sweet thoughts about their visiting detective. Nothing could be further from the truth. Well, not nothing. Ridley was a fascinating man. There was intelligence in his eyes, and he wasn't a man to suffer fools gladly.

Vivian pulled into the main gate of the Wallisford Hall property and they drove down a long straight road leading up to the house itself. Dory was more than glad she hadn't had to walk all this way. It would have taken her a couple of hours. Well, maybe an hour and a half. It wouldn't be so bad if she had a bicycle, but she didn't.

The car pulled up along the gravel until it came to a stop. Vivian got out and walked around the car, but Dory sorted herself before he actually came to help her. Instead, he leaned on the bonnet of the car, looking relaxed and utterly assured of himself. Dory supposed he was a man, and had been a child, who had always gotten what he wanted, and expected the same. "Well, Miss Sparks, you may ride in my car anytime you wish to."

A playful look lingered in his eyes and a slow smile turned up the corners of his mouth. That look automatically made Dory blush again. He was flirting with her, perhaps even waiting for her to make a suggestion for the next time he should take her out, which would be a deliberate outing. It was hard to tell if he was serious, or simply trying his luck for effect? Was this what he did with girls, tested how much they wanted to spend time with him? Obviously, he had no qualms about making assignations with the staff.

"If I find myself stranded somewhere in a horrible storm, I might take you up on the offer."

His smile widened and she didn't know if it was what she'd said, or the fact that she was effectively turning him down. She could well imagine it wasn't something that happened often. Then again, she didn't step out with any young man who asked her, and that included the young lords of the manor.

Chapter 8

Vivian Fellingworth's easy manner and winning smile lingered in her thoughts as she returned to her room. It surprised her how easily he overlooked the difference in their status—she a servant, and he a member of the family. There was something very uncomfortable about it. Not for a moment did she think it was her force of personality that moved him to make such an offer; rather, he was looking to spend time with any girl impressed with him.

Quite a few would fall for his charm, Dory assumed. Likely, he was the type to charm until he got what he wanted. The type wasn't entirely the purview of the upper classes—they existed everywhere. His fancy car and respectable name probably made him very successful at it. And the ease in which he slipped into flirting showed that it was an ingrained habit.

Dory busied herself in her room doing things she'd been hoping to do all week, including glancing through the magazine she'd just bought, eating her lollies and generally keeping off her feet.

Noise invaded the hall outside, signifying the other girls had arrived back. Getting up, Dory answered the door, seeing both Clara and Mavis in their smart Sunday clothes. "How was Aylesbury?"

"Marvelous," Clara said.

"Saw a movie with Clark Gable. Isn't he a dream. I will certainly dream about him tonight, I'm sure." Mavis giggled. Most likely, there had been a drink or two before coming home.

"It really was good. You should have come."

"I think I will next time."

"One day in Quainton is all you need, really. Although Nora did like to spend her time there. The shopkeeper said he saw her often."

"She was actually very secretive about what she got up to on her days off, always running off. She had a beau, you know, or at least she said she did," Clara said.

"Did you tell DI Ridley this?"

"Of course I did. Why would I hide something like that? But I don't know who it was. She never let on. Nora did like to keep her secrets. It was almost as if she prided herself on knowing things and not letting others know what. She was very annoying that way."

"That's ungenerous," Mavis said. "She was just a private person. Not all of us want everyone to know our business."

"What business have you to know about?"

"You mean besides the steamy romance between me and Clark Gable?"

"That would be the day. Enjoy those dreams of yours." Mavis walked off to her room.

"Larry thought it was a right shame you didn't come along," Clara continued, leaning against the wall with her ankle crossed over the other.

"Larry thinking that's a shame makes me less willing to come along."

"He's a nice boy."

"Aren't they all," Dory said sarcastically.

"They are all incorrigible flirts, aren't they?"

"Speaking of flirts, Vivian Fellingworth gave me a ride back from the village," Dory said, mainly to see how Clara reacted.

"Oh?" Clara said questioningly. "Might be the biggest flirt of all. Don't take it seriously. I suspect he's trying to make it a profession to flirt with girls. Charms them right out of their knickers, that one."

"I suspected as much."

"If you tip your hat in that direction, be aware of it."

"I have no intention to."

"I've heard that before as well."

"Like with Nora? Did she have interests in that direction?" Dory asked.

"Not that I saw. Then again, she did keep things close to her chest. They could have had a torrid affair for all I know. She was definitely stepping out with someone. What other reason could she have for spending every day off in Quainton?"

Massaging the nape of her neck, Dory considered the question, wondering if something very ugly lay underneath all this. A liaison gone wrong wasn't out of the realm of possibility, particularly if Nora started making demands of a reticent beau. Surely, she hadn't been pregnant? DI Ridley had said nothing of the kind, but then she knew from detective stories that they often kept things back, things only the people involved would know.

Was the charming golden boy secretly a murderer? Dory shuddered at the thought. Actually, she found it hard to imagine. He'd been easy to talk to, and not as stuck on propriety and tradition as some of the other people were in this house. No doubt, Mrs. Parsons would likely tan her backside if she knew the candid conversation they'd had during the ride back from Quainton. According to Mrs. Parsons, Dory should probably not have accepted the ride home at all, it being unseemly for someone in her position to accept favors with one of the family.

*

Come the evening, her day off had officially ended and she went to help Lady Pettifer prepare for supper.

"How was your day, Lady Pettifer?" Dory asked as she arrived at the older woman's room.

"A lovely day, wasn't it? Not too hot, but clear and cool. Days like this I don't miss France quite as much. Unfortunately, it is not every day we have such stunning weather, is it? If only we did, I would move back permanently."

"I take it you are staying over the summer?"

"Yes. I do prefer the summers here. It gets much too hot near the Mediterranean. Unbearably so."

Dory had a hard time imagining. The hot days she had ever known here in England were the loveliest days of her life. It was hard to imagine it being too hot. "There you are," Dory said, setting the last pin in Lady Pettifer's hair. "I'm sorry I'm not better at this."

"Never mind. I am too old to be vain. Why don't you walk down with me? See that I don't fall."

"Of course." They were not supposed to use the family staircase unless they were cleaning it, but it was a direct request from a family member. Mr. Holmes might not see that though. Lady Pettifer took Dory's offered arm.

"At my age, you become less stable on your feet."

They wandered leisurely down the hall and then downstairs. Dory helped Lady Pettifer to her seat, then rushed through the servants' door under the sternly watchful eye of Mr. Holmes.

Roast pork was on the menu tonight and Dory's stomach roared its delight as soon as the wafting smell hit her. "I really should learn some of your skill while I am here," she said to her aunt as she reached the kitchen.

"Learning how to cook a good meal is a gift you should give yourself." Gladys had finished with the main meal and was already working on dessert—some kind of meringue with cream and fruit.

Carrying the tray up with Clara, Dory returned to the dining room. Cedric was talking about some cricket match he'd played at Milton Common, catching up with some of his friends.

"You certainly will miss your Cambridge days," Lord Wallisford said to Vivian. "You don't quite appreciate them as much when you're there as you do after—when settled into your everyday life."

"I'm not planning on settling for anything," Vivian said, sitting casually with a drink in his hand.

Mr. Holmes carved the roast and Clara prepared the vegetables and gravy. Dory served, starting with Lord and Lady Wallisford, then Lady Pettifer who thanked Dory with a pat on her arm. Then the sons and the two visitors who were still at the house—one Cedric had brought with him from his cricket match, and another, who Dory couldn't tell exactly why they were here. Then again, it wasn't her place to question such things.

Lady Wallisford flustered dismissively at Vivian's comment. "You can't run around like a child all your life, can you? You really need to turn your mind to what you're going to do now. We can always set you up with a position at the home office, can't we, dear?" she questioned her husband.

"Sounds thrilling." The sarcasm was evident in Vivian's voice.

"You can't stay home the rest of your life."

"Why not? One does uncover some surprising things here every once in a while." That was an odd statement and Dory looked over to see him looking at her with a smile on his face. She didn't smile back.

His eyes followed her as she served around the table, and when she eventually raised her eyebrows in response to his blatant regard, he winked at her, taking another large swig from his glass. Next, she had to serve him and she half expected a pinch on her bottom and she gritted her teeth waiting for it, but it didn't come. Perhaps pinching girls' bottoms in front of his mother was a step too far, even for him.

Lady Wallisford's attention was on her too now as if she'd guessed the direction of Vivian's thoughts. A distressed blush colored Dory's cheeks. The unspoken accusation was unfair and unfounded. Vivian didn't seem to care how his badly disguised insinuations would affect her, the trouble he could get her into. One thing was sure: she had to watch out for him. Nothing about him alleviated the theory that he could have had an affair with Nora Sands. Could be he was simply moving onto his next conquest. Over her dead body would she fall for that one.

Chapter 9

"**V**ivian was acting a little queer last night," Lady Pettifer said, surveying Dory through the mirror of the dressing table. So that hadn't gone unnoticed by Lady Pettifer either.

"I think he was having a joke at my expense," Dory said. "He offered me a ride back from the village yesterday, and thinking of the long walk back, I accepted."

"I hope you don't have the propensity for being a silly girl."

"Not when it comes to silly boys, Lady Pettifer," Dory said with a firm glance through the mirror. "Not my game."

"I'm glad to hear it. Vivian can be very charming. A bit of a rascal, if you know what I mean. I shouldn't fall for it if I were you."

"I have no intention to." Dory was still smarting from the ease with which Vivian had bandied with her character the previous night. It had all been a bit of a joke, but jokes had the propensity to hurt someone—in this case, her.

"He's a lovely boy," Lady Pettifer continued. "Still so young. Out of all of them, my Andrew included, he was always the most boisterous. Probably because he was the youngest and always wanted to fit in with Cedric and Andrew. Always in such a rush to experience life." Lady

Pettifer put her powder brush down on the table. "Honoria always worries about him, and granted, out of the boys, his future is a little less secured."

In a way, it seemed strange that the fine, entitled people of these massive houses were worried for their children. Mothers were mothers, Dory supposed, and worried about their children no matter how endless their means. Still, it was unlikely Vivian would ever starve.

"He was here when Nora Sands was murdered, I believe. That must have been very difficult for him," Dory said, hanging up one of the ladyship's dresses into the wardrobe.

"Obviously a shock for everyone, but he seems to have taken it in his stride. Not sure he takes such things to heart."

"They weren't friends, then?"

"Vivian and that girl? Heavens, no. Why would he be? Granted, there were times when he was younger that he'd had an attraction to one of the servant girls, but what boy doesn't just as they are blooming into adulthood." Lady Pettifer sniffed as if she found the topic distasteful. "Vivian has a wide social circle, running off to house parties every other weekend. Nora Sands wouldn't hold any attraction for him now."

And yet, Lady Pettifer had noticed him paying attention to a servant girl last night at supper. Dory wasn't entirely sure what to believe. Something didn't ring true.

"Vivian is a lovely boy. He would never do anything to hurt someone." It was as if Lady Pettifer had read her thoughts. "That detective will find the culprit and all this suspicion will cease. This murder has the whole house on edge. It is so awful."

For a moment, Dory felt ashamed of her suspicions. She couldn't deny that she had them. "Let's hope he completes his investigation soon."

While DI Ridley was apparently on the property, Dory had little opportunity to speak to him. She was either required or he was off somewhere difficult to find. No one seemed to have any kind of tabs on him, and who really knew what policemen got up to as part of their quests.

A few moments later, she saw him in the garden from Lady Pettifer's window. "Speaking of, there he is."

"In the garden?" Lady Pettifer said and rose from her chair. "What is he doing in the garden?"

"Perhaps establishing if it's possible someone could have come in from outside?"

"Through the roses?"

"A murderer is unlikely to care about trampled roses."

"I can't see any trampled roses."

"You do have a point there, Lady Pettifer."

"I wonder if he's concluded anything."

"Nora Sands had a beau, you know," Dory said, "but she was very secretive about it."

The concerned look on Lady Pettifer's face showed that she was concerned about this new development. "It wasn't Vivian."

"Until the man is uncovered, suspicions are likely to fall everywhere."

"Go see if he's learned anything," Lady Pettifer suggested.

"I'm sure he won't tell me, but there is no harm in trying."

Dory rushed downstairs to intercept him before he disappeared again. What exactly he was doing was hard to tell. He seemed to be still staring at the roses.

"DI Ridley," she said with a small cough.

Looking up, he turned to her. "Miss Sands."

"I was speaking to the girls yesterday, the maids."

"I have spoken to them myself." There was a bored expectation in his voice as if he found this a little tedious.

"Then they mentioned that Nora Sands had a beau?"

"They did."

"It's curious, she was so secretive about it."

"Not sure it is all that curious," he said. "Some like to keep such things quiet."

"Vivian Fellingworth has a habit of flirting with the servant girls," Dory said, feeling disloyal to Lady Pettifer, but she had to say it. It was true. From what Lady Pettifer implied, he'd obviously been caught in some improper romance in his youth, and he had certainly flirted with her.

DI Ridley tilted his head slightly. "He failed to mention that when I spoke to him."

"Well, he would, wouldn't he?"

"Thank you for bringing this to my attention." It was dismissive in tone.

"Any developments?" Her attention turned to the roses.

"Hard to say there is anything that points to a specific direction at the moment. Establishing how many people had the means to commit the act is still fuzzy, and no hint of a motive yet."

Dory was surprised he was at all forthcoming. "It must have to do with this beau, surely?"

"Can't say. But you and Nora seemed to have something in common in that you are both very curious girls."

Dory closed her mouth. Was she being admonished?

"Vivian Fellingworth doesn't have an alibi, though, so it might be worth taking another look at his predilections." With a nod, DI Ridley walked away. Dory now had to go back and report that she had learned very little.

*

Vivian Fellingworth was called in for questioning in the study that afternoon. Dory was polishing one of the hall tables and dearly wished she could be in there. How exciting would it be to be a part, to observe? Obviously, she could listen in at the door, but there was a good chance that Mr. Holmes or Mrs. Parsons would catch her, and after Vivian's unguarded and blatant attention, she could not afford to put a step wrong.

Lady Pettifer was having tea with Lady Wallisford and Livinia, the daughter who had just arrived that morning.

Moving closer to the study door, Dory could only hear mumbling inside. Vivian's chuckle fleeted through, which suggested it wasn't an overly contentious discussion. What proof was there that there had been a relationship between him and Nora? How did one prove such a thing, unless Nora had told someone or written about it in a diary?

Then again, if she spent time in the village, then that had to be where the proof was.

Dory jumped as the door opened sharply and Vivian walked out, ignoring her. He looked cool with a drawn mouth. Obviously, not feeling flirtatious anymore. Seemed his interest in her only flared to life when it suited him.

DI Ridley emerged and he did look her way. The look on his face suggested he hadn't gotten what he wanted. He wandered off without being in a particular hurry and Dory returned to her work, spreading wood polish and rubbing it in until the wood gleamed. It was a task that tended to get her lost in her own thoughts out of sheer boredom. For that reason, she didn't strictly mind.

"Why did that ridiculous man feel he had to question him again?" the sharp tones of Lady Wallisford were heard drifting into the hall. "Are we forever going to suffer his presence?"

"Thank you, Holmes," Vivian's voice was heard. "I think he was insinuating that I had some romantic interest in the girl."

"What a ridiculous notion."

"I told him, and it's more or less true, I barely even noticed her. I don't wish to speak ill of the dead, but she wasn't exactly the type you notice, was she?"

"It's like that man is intent in his hope that this has something to do with us. He is wasting his time and ours, skulking around the house at all hours, giving flight to his hopes of pinning this on some person of means. It is a crime they let such men into the police in the first place."

"He is only doing his job, Hortense," Lady Pettifer said. "After all, someone did murder the girl."

Footsteps made her furiously rub the wood paneling in front of her after stopping to listen to the conversation in the parlor. Mr. Holmes appeared, looking down his nose at her when he saw her.

"Almost done," Dory said with a smile.

Chapter 10

Nothing was seen of DI Ridley for a few days and Dory was starting to wonder if he had given up on his investigation, the culprit never to be found. That would be a devastating shame for Nora's family, who would want to know what had happened to their daughter and why.

The activities in the house went on without him. The day of a maid was largely the same from one day to another. The general work in the mornings, cleaning out fireplaces, tidying and cleaning. Deal with Lady Pettifer's rise in the morning, then serve lunch, clean or polish something, then lastly, serve supper.

Amongst the family, Vivian left shortly after Livinia arrived, who spent much of her day on horseback. Cedric came and went. Most of the family members went their separate ways during the days, returning only for meals. Sometimes the house was entirely empty of family.

In fact, the days were quite tedious, Dory found. Maybe she would enjoy working in the kitchen with her aunt, Dory had started to wonder as she often spent long stretches of the day by herself. Dealing with Lady Pettifer was the most enjoyable part of the day because she liked to talk about her observations, her experiences and was genuinely interested in what Dory thought. As much as Dory loved Gladys and vice versa, Gladys never had time—

or inclination, it had to be said—to talk. It was a superfluous activity in the woman's mind. Lady Pettifer was a bit of a gossip.

Livinia, it turned out, was already engaged to a fine, young man from Kent. She spent most of her time in London with her acquaintances, doing things young ladies should do, which involved a fair bit of tea, shopping, dancing, weekends in the country and fine restaurants. Dory noticed that she showed absolutely no interest in the serving staff, not even acknowledging them when a teacup was handed to her. It was as if her supper plate simply appeared before her. For this reason, Dory couldn't warm to the girl, not that it was her place to have an opinion of the family members. Mostly, it was a burden on Mavis, who had to serve both Lady Wallisford and Livinia.

Mavis sat exhausted at the dining table when Dory made her way down for lunch. Lunch was served at one p.m. sharp and being late garnered a pinched look from either Mr. Holmes or Mrs. Parsons.

Gladys was already seated, her cheeks rosy from the heat of the kitchen. Dory smiled at her as she took her seat.

"Gossip in the village says that the detective has found Nora's boyfriend," Larry said, taking the steaming bowl of potatoes.

Shocked gasps sounded around the table.

"Who?" Clara said.

"Michael Jones. Or so they say."

"The mechanic?" Clara asked. This was obviously unexpected news. "Why didn't she ever say?"

Dory had never heard of Michael Jones, the mechanic.

"I wonder if he is being grilled by Ridley right as we speak. They say if you are murdered, the highest chance is that it's someone you know, the closer the more likely."

Clara visibly shuddered. "I am never getting married."

Mr. Holmes cleared his throat. "It serves no one to tattle about such things. We will leave it to the police to perform their duties."

This new development threw a spanner in all of Dory's theories. She had been completely wrong suspecting Vivian was the person responsible, or at least the person Nora had been meeting with. Suddenly, she felt ungenerous, and even that her activities had been dangerous. She had gone completely in the wrong direction.

"Goes to show you never know someone," Mavis stated. "I've known Michael Jones all my life. We were at school together. He was a couple years ahead, but still."

"Just because he was dating her doesn't automatically mean he killed her," Larry said, a harsh look on his face. He obviously didn't like the insinuation on Michael Jones' behalf.

Mr. Holmes cleared his throat, suggesting he wanted no more discussion on the offending topic, so they ate in silence. Any further discussion would likely result in rebuke, but they were all now stewing in their own thoughts. After lunch, they were dismissed and sent on their way to their afternoon duties.

Dory decided to go in search for Lady Pettifer, who tended to spend a bit of time in her room after lunch. Hopefully, she wasn't sleeping, but Dory knew that Lady Pettifer would want to know about this latest development at the earliest opportunity. Out of all the family, Lady Pettifer was intensely interested in what had happened to poor Nora.

Knocking lightly on the door, she was told to enter, and found Lady Pettifer was lying on the bed, peeping out from under her satin sleeping eye mask.

"I can come back later," Dory said, barely louder than a whisper.

"No, what is it?"

"Well," Dory said, stepping into the room and closing the door behind her. "Turns out Nora Sand's boyfriend has been found. A mechanic in the village by the name of Michael Jones."

Sitting up, Lady Pettifer stroked her knuckles under her chin. "A mechanic, you say. From the village. That is interesting, isn't it?"

"I understand some of the people downstairs know him."

"So, a boy from the village. That is certainly a development. Perhaps this means we are a step closer to finding this killer. I suppose we will know in a day or two if DI Ridley makes an arrest."

"It could be he's very close, but from what I have observed, he is very measured in his actions," Dory said. In truth, she had no reference to judge his competence by, but he was serious in nature, and that surely signified a competent man. Well, she hoped so. "I will leave you to rest."

"I think I will sleep better now."

Dory hadn't realized that this murder was so disconcerting for Lady Pettifer, but why wouldn't it be? A murderer around wasn't comfortable for anyone. Withdrawing, she made her way downstairs to beat the rugs from the upstairs guest rooms while the weather was still holding. On the wireless, they had said bad weather was coming down from the north in the next few days, which meant that it would probably be raining on her day off.

The air was brisk and the sun warming when she walked outside. There was definitely a sense of spring without the real warmth of summer. A bar served as a whipping post and Dory grabbed the woven cane beater after manhandling the rugs up.

Clouds of dust plumed with every beat and Dory began to cough. This was not the most glamorous part of her job. Actually, she didn't know if there was a glamorous part. This certainly wasn't the highlight.

As she worked, she saw the sporty, white car Vivian drove coming down the long road to the house. It appeared Vivian was back, which meant there would be the full complement of family for supper that night.

Pulling around, he got out of the car, wearing a cream-colored suit, looking smart as he always did. Well, for now, Vivian was off the hook—at least it appeared so. It was hard to think of Cedric in the role of Lothario. It just seemed too ill-suited to his staid and colorless personality. At least Vivian was a charmer. If Cedric charmed, it wasn't something he did at home. In fact, Dory wasn't entirely sure he liked women in any respect. He certainly didn't seek their company if he could avoid it. There was no talk of a girlfriend or a fiancée, but maybe he was like Nora in that regard and kept everything close to his chest.

*

"It appears a boyfriend for that girl has been found," Cedric said around the table as the family waited to be served. Candles cast light around the table, but the rest of the room seemed particularly dark that night, which meant that Lady Wallisford had a headache. The woman didn't look worse for wear, but she never did, Dory had learnt. In fact, she never left her room looking less than respectable.

Vivian looked bored. "About time," he said.

"Can you believe?" Lady Wallisford started with amusement in her voice. "That ridiculous policeman suspected our Vivian was seeing her on the side?"

Lord Wallisford harrumphed, but his attention was more for the plate of sole, capers and cream being placed down in front of him.

Vivian seemed uninterested in dining and smoked, looking formal in his dark suit, his hair slicked back with a darker hue than usual.

Livinia's laugh was tinkling and laced with a degree of venom. "Well, Vivian is interested in anything wearing a skirt, so it's hardly surprising, is it? That should teach you, Vivian. If there is a murder, they will automatically look at you."

Vivian made a face to say he wasn't amused. In fact, he seemed unusually grumpy that night. Before, he had been overly attentive to Dory, now he didn't acknowledge her when she put his plate down. Hopefully Mr. Holmes noticed that, too.

"If Vivian is going to stick something in a girl, it's hardly going to be a knife," Cedric said, his voice thin and brittle.

"Cedric!" Lady Wallisford chided, but Livinia laughed. "I will not have that kind of talk around the dining table." Lord Wallisford chuckled. If anyone managed this family, it was Lady Wallisford. Her husband tended to keep quiet and enjoyed the incorrigible antics of his children more than he chided them.

Chapter 11

Sunshine made Dory ache to be outside. It felt as though she had been inside all winter, and now she longed to be outside. The gardeners had to love days like this. But for her, there was little opportunity. Perhaps she would sit out by the kitchen garden for a few minutes after lunch.

Lady Pettifer was taking advantage of the sunshine, going for a walk along the property, and Livinia was out riding as usual. In truth, Dory was impressed because she was frightened of horses herself, seeing them as unpredictable and crushingly large. But it had to be exciting going full tilt on the back of one in an unrestrained gallop. Most likely, she would never know.

Dory carried down the last of the family's lunch, which had been conducted in near silence that day, attended only by Lady Pettifer and Lord Wallisford. The silence between the siblings was a comfortable one, though. Everyone else had chosen to spend the day away. Maybe the fine weather had them all seeking to get out of the house as well.

The downstairs was noisy as the staff gathered for lunch. As above, once seated, it was a silent affair, many finishing as quickly as they could to return to work or to steal a few moments for themselves, like Dory was going to do.

She sought the bench outside which sat along the wall of the house in the full view of the sun, where she stretched out her legs and absorbed as much sun as she could.

The seat creaking next to her suggested someone had joined her and she opened her eyes to see Larry rolling a cigarette from his pouch of tobacco. He looked troubled, his brow drawn tight.

"What's the matter, Larry?"

He didn't speak for a moment. "This business with Michael Jones. It doesn't sit right. I went to school with him. Always a big teddy bear, you know? Not a mean bone in his body. Granted, not the brightest spark out there, but he'd never hurt anyone. I can't see him coming up here and stabbing Nora. I just can't see it."

"You never really know what's in someone's heart," Dory said.

"Not with Michael Jones. What you see is what you get. I would bet my right arm that he has nothing to do with this. If he was stepping out with Nora, he'd be treating her well. It's just not right. If that's the way they're looking, they're barking up the wrong tree. I'll never believe Michael Jones is responsible for this."

"Convenient for someone if you are right," Dory said, feeling conflicted. Of course a friend would never see the blackness in someone which could lead them to kill, or could they? If she were asked, she couldn't readily point her finger at anyone she had met here and say that person had inside them what it took to take a life. Taking someone's life—it was such an alien concept, she couldn't wrap her mind around it.

In a sense, she wanted to believe that this Michael Jones was the culprit, predominantly because they would then have all the answers and there wouldn't be that uncomfortable feeling that someone sinister was hiding behind a smiling face. Villains didn't actually look like they were supposed to, with beady and cold eyes, dressed in black trench coats. No, someone was disguising themselves very well—whether it be Michael Jones or not.

With a sigh, Dory rose and returned to her duties. As she walked in the door, Mrs. Parsons told her that Lady Pettifer had rung her bell and Dory redirected herself to her mistress.

Lady Pettifer had risen from her nap and was sitting at the dressing table. "I miss my dog," she said. "My Beauty. She is always such a joy in my life."

"I never had a dog. My mam never liked them."

"Man's best friends, and that can't be argued. It is such a shame about the quarantine laws, but they won't budge. If I brought her, she'd have to sit in a cage the whole of summer. She must be pining for me. It is the worst thing about coming back for the summer. I think I shall go for a walk before supper. I do so enjoy dusk."

Dory went to the wardrobe and pulled out Lady Pettifer's preferred walking coat.

"What is the matter with you? You look glum today."

Dory sighed again. "Not glum, exactly. It's this business with Michael Jones. Larry, the gardener, knows him well and says it would be completely out of his character to do something like this."

"Can't always trust someone's opinion of character."

"That was what I said, but Larry wouldn't have it. Said with Michael Jones, you get what you see."

"Well, I am sure that DI Ridley will sort it out. By nature of being the girl's beau, it is only natural that he is questioned."

"Of course," Dory said and helped Lady Pettifer dress. A simple brushing was all she wanted, before pinning her hat. It was one thing Dory didn't feel comfortable doing, running a sharp hat pin along someone's scalp.

"I'll see you at supper," Lady Pettifer said before she left, grabbing her walking stick perched in the corner of the room.

*

With aching feet, Dory sat down at the servants' dinner table later that night after finishing serving the family supper. Tiredness had set in and she ached for Sunday when she could sleep in and even do nothing at all. Obviously, that would only be for an hour before she grew bored, but how she longed for that hour right now.

"They've arrested Michael Jones," said George Henry, the chauffeur, as he sat down at the table, putting his uniform hat in his lap.

A gasp spread around the table and Larry looked thunderous.

"They have to have it wrong," Mavis said. "Michael Jones wouldn't hurt anyone." It seemed Mavis' testaments to his character was the same as Larry's. "It will be a travesty of justice if they pin this on him."

"Well, they had to have some reason, don't they?" George challenged. "They wouldn't just arrest him with no evidence at all."

"Been known to happen," Larry countered, sitting with a scowl on his face and his arms crossed. "Wouldn't be the first time. I'm sure they've hung innocent men and all."

"Poor Michael," Mavis said, a worried expression on her face. "This is awful. They won't hang him, surely."

"There would have to be a trial first," Mr. Holmes said. "If he is guilty there, then he will hang, and it will be the end of it."

"Not when the real murderer gets away with it. Who's to say they won't do it again? Maybe we are all at risk of being murdered in our beds," Mavis said, a hint of hysteria in her voice.

Dory hadn't guessed this news would have such a devastating effect around the table. It was certainly divisive and some were now questioning the effectiveness of the justice system in general. For herself, she didn't know what to think. Both Larry and Mavis, who knew Michael Jones, didn't doubt his innocence, and why would he come up to the house to murder his girlfriend?

Well, he certainly wouldn't do it at his house, but why here? Down some dark alley, maybe, but to sneak into a large hall and commit murder?

Savagely chewing her nail, Dory looked around the table. Everyone looked uncomfortable with this news. The people who knew him said this was incorrect, while others probably wanted a culprit, any culprit, to be found. Hanging the wrong man, though, that would be tough to live with when the truth really did come out.

Dory was one who believed the truth always came out in the end. It was a mantra her mother used to raise her children by, and over time, that mantra had always proved true. Any wrongdoing always got back to the doer in the end.

After supper, Dory returned to the bench outside along the kitchen garden. It was dark as black ink outside, but she just felt like she needed some air. Even she had to admit that something felt very wrong about this. But perhaps it wasn't. She didn't know the things that DI Ridley knew. It could be that he had concrete proof and this man was responsible. In a way, she hoped not, because she didn't want Larry and Mavis, who knew this man well, to be unable to tell that this person was deceptively dark and despicable. How was anyone supposed to know anyone if you couldn't trust your own judgment?

Chapter 12

"Well, so speak to him, girl, if all you can do is worry," Lady Pettifer said.

"Who?"

"DI Ridley. He seems a sensible man and I'm sure he didn't just accuse a man because it was convenient."

"If he thinks he has his man, he is unlikely to come here anytime soon. In fact, he will probably leave the village in short order if he hasn't already."

"Then go see him if you can't settle your mind."

"I can't just go see him. I have duties. It would take half a day to walk to the village and back."

"True, you do have duties. There is a bicycle in the garage, upon which you can go to the village and get me some sherbets. The great compensation for getting older, dear, is that you can rightfully insist on being unreasonable. Now, go. I want my sherbets."

"Are you sure?"

"Yes. Let me know what the man says and we shall see what evidence he has."

At this point, Dory knew that Lady Pettifer was as interested in knowing about the investigation of this murder as she was. "I will ride like the wind."

A quick wave of Lady Pettifer's fingers and Dory was gone, rushing downstairs after getting her coat and beret. The lady wanted sherbets—who was she to argue.

82

"Aunt Gladys," she said as she entered the kitchen, thinking she should tell someone.

"And where are you off to?"

"Lady Pettifer has asked me to bike down to the village to get her some sherbets."

Gladys raised her eyebrows. "I'm not sure you should be used in that way."

"She had missed them so much in her time in France, I hadn't the heart to say no." Lying wasn't something she was entirely comfortable with, but it was an innocent lie and there was potentially an innocent man at risk. "I will ride like the wind."

"See that you do. Mrs. Parsons won't be happy about this."

"Maybe I can get back before she notices."

"Nothing gets past that woman."

Walking over to kiss her aunt on the cheek, she continued to the door. "I will be as fast as I can. Do you need anything?"

"Might as well get me some sherbets, too."

Dory smiled. "I probably shouldn't tell anyone else or I will be overburdened with confectionaries on the way home."

She ran to the garage and opened the door. Sure enough, there was an old but serviceable bicycle leaning up against one of the walls, which she led outside and set off. It had been a while, so she wasn't entirely stable at first, until she picked up some speed. Then she pedaled like fire was racing up behind her, glad she had brought her coat because the wind was cool at speed.

It took about half an hour to get to town and Dory went straight to the pub, looking in the window to see if DI Ridley was there. Luckily for her, he was nursing a pint in the late afternoon.

"Hello again, Mr. Ridley," she said, walking in with her beret in hand. "What a coincidence seeing you here again." She really was getting terribly good with her little white lies. Perhaps that was not something to be proud of.

"Miss Sparks," he said, looking up from his paper.

"Rumor has spread around the hall that you have made an arrest."

"So we have," he said after returning his pint to the table.

"The mechanic in the village."

"Yes," he confirmed grudgingly.

"Of course, the people who know him say you are barking up the wrong tree with him, the sweetest man you would ever meet."

"Are you interrogating me, Miss Sparks?"

The idea shocked her. "No, of course not." Maybe she actually was. "Perhaps I just wanted to let you know that there are quite a few who know him, who believe it is not in his character."

The man sighed and folded his paper. "I can tell you aren't going to leave this be. We found a bloody rag at his shop."

Dory's eyes widened.

"It is human blood."

"He is a mechanic. Injuries as part of the profession."

"Well, he could not present a cut of any kind."

"So he ran up to the hall, because surely, it would have been noted if he drove there, stabbed Miss Sparks and then ran what had to be a good hour and a half to his garage to clean his hands on a rag as if no one would ever look there, bypassing a multitude of streams along the way?"

"Or discarded a rag he had in his pocket," DI Ridley said. There was a tightness around his mouth that suggested he wasn't pleased.

"The rag could have been there days before, or even days after the murder. How does he explain it?"

"He said he had a nosebleed."

Dory was stunned. "Is this sufficient grounds to charge him?"

"It obviously is since I did."

"It is pretty circumstantial evidence to hang a man by."

"The arrest, Miss Sparks, is a more preventative measure until we find more evidence either for or to the contrary. We cannot have him run at this point. Accused men have a habit of doing that—innocent or not."

"So you are not convinced he is guilty?"

"You have a habit of interrogating me, Miss Sparks. Do you fancy yourself an amateur sleuth?"

"Don't be preposterous," she stated. "I just grow concerned when the people around me are so adamant that he is innocent."

"There are always people who are adamant about someone's innocence, no matter what they have done. He could have been seen doing the actual murder and someone would say he was innocent."

Well, he had her there. "I am sorry, but I think we all need to pay attention when a man's life is on the line, and a woman's forfeit."

"Thank you for your concern and vigilance, Miss Sparks, but please don't make assumptions. The investigation is far from concluded. But yes, it is unlikely that a man travel such a far distance to murder someone on a whim. Usually, an unobserved murder involving such distances would involve something meticulously planned. Murder is rarely well planned. In fact, it is rarely planned at all, simply a reaction."

Dory found herself absorbing everything he said. His insight was fascinating. "If that were true, it would suggest someone at the house."

"Yes," Ridley said and lit a cigarette, the acrid smoke billowing over the table and into the air.

"You have not given up on investigating the people at the house."

"Except you, Miss Sparks. Somehow I can't see you having a strong enough ambition to murder for your current role."

"Pfft," she said dismissively. "I'm more likely to murder to get out of it." He raised his eyebrows. "Figure of speech, of course. I would actually never murder anyone."

"Everyone can be induced to murder if the circumstances are right."

It was a chilling thought and he said it with such certainty, Dory had no doubt he believed it. What things had this man seen in his career; she shuddered at the thought.

"So, I take it we will see you at the hall again?"

"Probably very soon. In the meantime, no harm is being done to Michael Jones in our cells. In fact, it might serve the investigation if the real murderer believes they have gotten away with it."

Dory nodded, seeing the logic of it.

"Of course, it will serve very little," he continued, "if you go around and speak of it to all and sundry."

"I won't," she assured him, knowing that Lady Pettifer would want to know everything he said. As she had not been present, or even in the country, when the murder happened, it could not have been her. But she did see the sense in not divulging anything of this to anyone. How she was going to deal with Lady Pettifer was something she would have to consider on the way. "I had better run. On an errand."

Rising, she gave the detective a nod before slipping away. She could feel him watching her. Likely he found her a professional annoyance, but he had taken her into his confidence to some degree—probably to shut her up. She would not betray him. There was too much riding on this for the innocent and victimized.

Grabbing the bicycle by the handles, she walked over to the general merchant, thoughts racing around her head with what she'd learnt. DI Ridley firmly thought someone at the house was responsible and his logic was hard to fault—which meant she, and Gladys, were living under the same roof as a murderer. She would definitely be locking her door that night, and every night after until the person was caught. Still, Nora had been murdered for a reason and they had no idea why.

Chapter 13

Sherbets in her pocket, Dory cycled back to Wallisford Hall, thoughts still racing through her mind about the things DI Ridley had said. It seemed, he, too, did not think Michael Jones was responsible for the murder. But he also thought someone at the hall was. In her mind, Dory went through all the people there, trying to see any reason one of them would kill Nora Sands, but nothing presented itself.

Noise assaulted her with the force of a wave, stunning her as she sat perched on top two wheels. Her front wheel veered off and she just about lost her balance when a car zoomed past her at speed. Wind blew grit in her face and a cloud of dust enveloped her.

"Damn it," she swore, trying to stabilize herself as she looked at the car speeding away down the road. Of course it was the sporty white car Vivian Fellingworth drove and she saw the back of his blond hair in the distance. Why had he driven past her so fast? Had he not noticed there was a bicyclist on the road? He'd just about driven her into a ditch. Not to mention that she was now covered in dust. Rude, boorish and uncouth.

That was him, though, wasn't it? Charming when he wanted to make an impression, boorish any other time. Dory had the urge to tell him exactly where he could stick his stellar personality—and his road skills. Unfortunately, once at the hall, it was not her place to tell him what she thought about anything. That was probably the part that grated the most about being in domestic service—the understanding that the family could behave any way they damned well pleased.

In burning fury, Dory rode home, still upset at nearly being run off the road. The offending vehicle stood haphazardly on the gravel in front of the house, just about blocking one of the other cars, the driver nowhere to be seen. Dory was of mind to actually hit him, which would probably get her fired. What were the chances that someone like him would take his just desserts with circumspection? Zero, she would guess.

Still grumbling, she walked down the external servants' stairs to the kitchen where Gladys was preparing pastry for the evening meal. "Vivian Fellingworth almost ran me off the road in that horrible car of his."

"He must not have seen you," Gladys said, fervently rolling her pastry.

"I was the only thing on the road," Dory complained. "How could he not see me?"

How could he *not* see her? How could one miss a bicyclist like that? Or did he? Either he didn't care, or maybe he was even *trying* to run her off the road. The thought was chilling. No, it couldn't be, she thought, dismissing the idea.

Hanging her coat up, she returned to the kitchen, but Mrs. Parsons was now there. "Isn't there something you should be doing?" she said sharply. "And why are you dressed without your uniform?"

"Lady Pettifer had me run an errand, but that task is completed now, so I just came to see if there is something particular you wish for me to do," Dory lied.

"Well, if you have run out of things to do. I think the library could use a dusting and some straightening."

"I'll get right on it," Dory said with a smile that she could see hadn't entirely alleviated Mrs. Parsons' suspicion.

After changing into her uniform, she returned downstairs to the family floor to carry out her work in the library.

"Well, if you won't do something about it, I will," she heard Cedric's curt voice.

Dory paused as she passed the door of the study.

"They can't just do what they want; there are consequences for such actions."

"Calm down, Cedric," the deep, slow voice of Lord Wallisford said. "I will make sure nothing comes of it."

Hearing footsteps, Dory hurried down the hall toward the library. The fire grate was clean, so no one had asked for the fire to be lit in the last day. There was perhaps a little dust, but not much. Bringing out her ostrich feather duster, Dory pulled the railed ladder over and climbed up to the top of the shelf, where a thin coating of dust had accumulated. No one would ever see the dust up here, but she had learned that the fact no one could see it didn't matter to Mrs. Parsons. If there was dust, it had to be removed, even if no one would ever be the wiser. It was as if dust, by simply being there, spoilt the atmosphere.

Marching footsteps sounded down the hall and then the front door slammed. Cedric's car roared to life and soon gravel was spraying across the driveway. Something had clearly upset Cedric. Dory went through the words she'd overheard. Someone was trying to get away with something and it was upsetting Cedric. Lord Wallisford obviously had the power to stop or influence them.

He had clearly said 'they,' and Dory didn't think it was family members ganging up on him—although she wouldn't necessarily put it past them, but she suspected this was referring to something else. Probably related to the steps Cedric was taking into parliamentary circles. As the oldest son, he would one day inherit the title, and hence, a place at the House of Lords.

Could any of this have anything to do with Nora's death? It was hard to see how. No one had suspected that Nora and Cedric had ever been anything more than respectful of their proper roles. It wasn't as if Nora had been pregnant and in some way able to blackmail him. Even if she were, no one would listen to some maid decrying her loose virtue. Besides, Cedric seemed to have no interest in the maids. That was Vivian's territory.

*

Cedric was sullen as the family dined that night, maybe even a little more relaxed than usual. Dory guessed he'd spent some time at the pub, or somewhere else where people drank. Who knew where he did such things. Hardly with the riff raff in Quainton's pub. From what she'd seen, Cedric liked sticking with his ilk.

As per usual, Vivian was decidedly relaxed as well, his eyes glazed in the candle light on the table. "Why don't we have some champagne, Holmes," he suggested.

"I'm sure you've had enough, Vivian," Lady Wallisford said tartly.

"Enough? But the night has barely started, and we do have things to celebrate, don't we?"

"Such as?" Cedric said in his driest voice.

"Well, you have made quite an impression at Parliament, I hear. That's something to celebrate."

Cedric turned beet red and his chin rose even higher than normal.

Dory ladled soup into the fine bone china bowls. It was a creamy bisque and it smelled heavenly. Hopefully they would have some downstairs later. Clara carried a steaming roast beef on a wooden platter to rest before carving. The smell of it made Dory's mouth water even more and her stomach growled.

Bringing the bowl of soup to Lord Wallisford, Dory put it down, while Clara followed with a basket of bread rolls, placing one on a small plate with a pair of silver tongs.

"Although some would argue not quite the impression you wanted to make. Was it, Cedric, the impression you wanted to make?" Vivian said, a sly smile twisting his lips in wry amusement. With raised eyebrows, he was devilishly handsome when he did that, but it was also pure arrogance, as if nothing could ever concern or touch him.

"Vivian," Lady Wallisford chided. "It is a step in the right direction."

Cedric's mouth was drawn so tight, it disappeared.

"What was it," Vivian said, apparently not content with roasting his brother, "special envoy to the Society of... Acoustics?"

"Audiology," Cedric said grudgingly, unhappily taking part in Vivian's goading.

"How riveting. They must have real belief in your capabilities, Brother. And not envoy, is it? They're actually trusted outside the country. No, you are... a coordinator?"

"Liaison," Cedric finally confirmed.

"It's an initial assignment; somewhere he can show what he's made of," Lord Wallisford said brusquely, steeling himself away from the soup.

"And what did Stephen Hedgestow get? Seconded to the League of Nations, wasn't he? And he's an idiot," Vivian continued with a snort.

"Audiology is of prime importance. We're heading into a war, but you wouldn't notice that, would you, Vivian, being but a schoolboy."

Cedric bit back, it seemed. Vivian's grin wasn't quite as wide, but he wasn't giving up.

"What are you going to make of your life?" Cedric continued, being on a roll. "Being a lush isn't an actual profession, and from what I hear, most of your tutors still don't know what you look like."

"Can't help being brilliant."

"At what?"

"Boys," Lady Wallisford cut in.

"Cedric is right," Lord Wallisford announced. "Your marks do leave quite a bit to be desired."

"Oh no, am I missing the opportunity to be a liaison to the Society of Orthodontics?"

Cedric's eyes narrowed. "I doubt the Society of Ornithologists would have you. Not interested in the dull and dim-witted birds you avail yourself to. Not all of us are interested in filling the English countryside with bastards."

"Cedric!" Lady Wallisford chided. "That will be enough."

Dory felt like rolling her eyes, but she had to carry herself with serenity—as if she was floating on a cloud, completely oblivious to the vicious snipes going on around her. Although, in a sense, she should be offended because she was one of the 'dull and dim-witted birds' Vivian had had an attempt at, when not trying to run her off the road. Oh, how she wanted to spill a whole bowl of bisque over his head. Mr. Holmes would probably suffer an apoplectic fit and die, and Dory didn't want that on her conscience.

Chapter 14

It felt like a blessing by the time Sunday rolled around. Dory went to church with the others, but she felt more lost and confused than ever. It couldn't be said that she liked her employers. Technically, Mrs. Parsons was her employer, but the Fellingworth family paid her wages and it was them she served. Could people really be so disagreeable? It made her wonder if it was wealth that spoiled people. It was hard to say it was some environmental quality. They had moral guidance the same as everyone else. In fact, they were sitting in the front pew. One would figure they would hear better than anyone else. It certainly wasn't lack of education.

Hopefully, it was some superficial quality that made them so disagreeable. Maybe it was just that they didn't have to be agreeable that caused it. Was that a natural disposition if one didn't have to get on with the people? Dory didn't know. But it was certainly not a done thing complaining about the family. Some degree of loyalty was expected, irrespective of how they behaved. At least enough not to talk about their foibles and shortcomings.

Dory had decided she didn't much like Vivian either. She had seen his charming side, but she had seen him without it, too, and it was definitely a mask he wore when he chose to.

As she had come to expect by now, DI Ridley was not in church today either. What she didn't know was if he had a day off like everyone else or if he simply kept going until the case was solved. Timeliness was supposedly important in a murder investigation, so perhaps he didn't have days off.

The reverend was talking about charity and the need to be merciful and generous with those who had little. From what she had seen of Quainton, there was no one here in real need, not like the stories one heard from London. Like in Swanley, everyone had a job and got on with it. Work was found for idle hands.

The service ended and they all streamed out to a lovely day. The last vestiges of winter were gone and it was downright summery. The breeze was a little cool, but flowers bloomed and the bees buzzed. It was a lovely picture; a lovely day.

"Are you coming to the pictures in the afternoon?" Mavis asked, wearing her navy jacket and pencil skirt. She looked very smart and Dory wished she had something similar. Perhaps she should buy some material in Aylesbury to make herself a new skirt.

"Why not?"

"Well, we're having lunch at the pub before we go. Larry wants a pint."

"Oh, alright," Dory said, feeling nervous tension rise up her with the mention, which was curious all on its own. The thought of seeing DI Ridley made her feel a little skittish. It was something that had come on just lately and she couldn't account for it—uncertain if it had to do with his temperate opinion of her and her curiosity, or more that she threatened to blush when he looked her in the eye.

So, they were off to the pub. It was a squeeze in the back seat of the car Larry drove and it soon grew warm. She would have to take her jacket and hat off before they set off for Aylesbury, or she would be a roasted mess by the time they got there.

The pub was as busy as Dory had seen it, but there was no DI Ridley in sight. Perhaps he had gone home for the day, maybe even to see his family. There was no ring on his finger, but not all men wore rings. It wasn't as if she had been blatant enough to ask.

A tiny, round table had to serve them while they had their pint of beer or glass of cider. Dory preferred a cider. The taste always reminded her of autumn.

"Stephen," Larry said, nodding to the large, young man sitting at the next table. "Michael home yet?"

"Not yet," the man said brusquely, sitting with his big, meaty arms crossed. His hair was light brown, the same color as his round eyes.

Larry blew a disapproving noise through his teeth. The Michael Larry was referring to had to be Michael Jones, which probably made this his brother. Dory smiled at him.

"It's shocking that they've arrested him," Mavis said. "Downright shocking."

"Yep," Stephen said and rose, walking over to the bar to get himself another pint.

"I might get some nuts," Dory said, feeling like something salty. Rising, she made her way over to the bar.

"Dory Sparks," she said, holding out her hand to Stephen, who stared at her for a moment before shaking her hand.

"I heard a rumor there was a new girl up at the house."

"Well, they were one short, it seems," she said uncomfortably. "I didn't find out about the nature of the vacancy before I arrived. I met the man who is investigating, though."

"Useless sack of shit," Stephen grumbled. "Couldn't find a piss up in a brewery, that one."

Dory wasn't sure that was true, but it wasn't her place to disclose anything DI Ridley had told her in confidence. "I am sorry about suspicion being placed with your brother. I'm sure that's not true."

"Damn right it's not true. My brother would never hurt Nora. He thought the world of that girl."

"She seemed to like him, too, considering she spent every weekend here in the village. But they seemed to keep their romance quite secret. Nora refused to tell anyone about it."

Stephen shrugged. "Some people don't like others in their business."

"Where did they meet? I'm assuming they didn't come here."

"At the workshop," Stephen said. "Well, I saw them at the workshop quite a bit. Sometimes they went out—went for drives."

"It's so sad what has happened. I feel so sorry for your brother. It would be hard to think that at any moment, it could be the last time you see someone. Makes you think."

"Mhh," he said, looking down on the bar.

"I never met her, of course, but I'm sorry I never knew her. She seemed like a nice girl."

"I suppose she would have been my sister-in-law in time." Stephen sounded really sad. There certainly didn't appear to be any contention in the Jones family regarding who their son was seeing.

"When was the last time you saw her?"

"In the workshop. She was there with Michael."

"Were they going for a drive?"

He seemed lost in thought for a moment. "No, they were staying there."

"Did she like cars, then?"

"No, not really. Although," he continued after a moment, "she was interested in some of Mike's work."

"Oh?"

"Something a while back. I can't remember, but she was asking questions about something Mike did to a car. I wasn't staying, so I don't really know what it was about."

This was odd, Dory thought. Why would Nora be interested in something like that? "Was there anything unusual Mike had worked on?"

"Nothing out of the ordinary. There was that blown gearbox in a tractor which was a hell of a job, but nothing unusual beyond that."

Picking up his pint, Stephen walked away to another part of the pub and Dory decided not to order another glass of cider.

"Well, I think we're just about ready to go," Larry said as Dory returned empty-handed to the table. Grabbing her bag and her jacket, she followed the others out to the car parked just down the road. Cars were parked on every available space outside the pub and people were still coming. Their table would have been claimed by a new group already, Dory suspected.

The drive to Aylesbury was long and winding, and the car was cramped in the back. Dory's shins were tight and her back ached by the time she stepped out again, not far from the market located in a large square. It was busy with people, and children ran around. An ice cream shop was off to the side and suddenly, Dory loved the idea of an ice cream.

"Picture theater is over there," Clara said, pointing in the other direction. A white board with black letters clearly showed where the theater was.

Dory sighed. "I thought I might actually go look for some cloth." She had changed her mind about spending the day inside the dark theater. Clara looked torn between going with her, or going to the pictures, which she really wanted. "You go to the pictures. I'll wait outside when you're done."

"If you're sure."

"Of course, I'm sure. Gives me a chance to familiarize myself with that ice cream parlor."

"The main street is down there," Clara said, indicating one of the streets running off the main square. "You should be able to find what you need there. If you're sure you don't mind?" Clara was eager to go.

"Go," Dory said, urging her away and Clara was off, catching up with Mavis, who was buying raspberries at one of the market stalls with Larry. They all spoke for a moment and Dory could see Clara telling the other two that she wasn't coming. Larry looked disappointed. He clearly still wanted to spend time with her, even though she had given him no encouragement.

Left to her own devices, Dory's thoughts returned to Nora and what Stephen had earlier said in the pub. Nora had been interested in something Michael Jones was doing in his workshop, which was enough out of character that Stephen commented on it. Did it mean something? She had no idea. Perhaps it was something she should tell DI Ridley about. But then, she might have annoyed him enough already.

Chapter 15

"How was Aylesbury?" Lady Pettifer asked. "I wish I was still young enough to run around a whole day."

"I think you could run circles around me if you wanted to," Dory said, hanging up Lady Pettifer's morning dress.

"Did you go to the pictures?"

"No, I wasn't in the mood to sit in a dark theater. It was too lovely a day. Besides, my mind was too distracted to pay attention to a movie."

"And what is it that distracts you?"

"Well, I met the brother of Michael Jones, the one DI Ridley arrested. He thought there was no chance that his brother would ever harm Nora, that he was crazy about her, intent on marrying her. And judging by how willing she was to spend time with him, it seems a stretch. Men with brutal natures tend to show it, don't they?" In Swanley, everyone knew about poor Patty with her bruiser of a husband. Everyone knew, everyone saw the evidence—no one was surprised by the state of their relationship. "And frankly… " She was just about to reveal what DI Ridley had said about him not thinking him guilty, either, but caught herself in time. He'd made her promise not to disclose what he'd said. Also, she now felt guilty for not telling Lady Pettifer such an important detail.

Lady Pettifer was silent for a moment, sitting in the white cane chair by the window with her discarded book in her lap. "I really have no idea who could have done this terrible thing," she confessed.

"I don't either," Dory said quietly, although she still didn't entirely dismiss Vivian, but Lady Pettifer didn't want to hear any suspicion cast on the boys. Even so, they seemed the most likely if DI Ridley's suspicions were true, that it was someone in the house. Dory sighed. "I think we can safely say it isn't Mr. Holmes or Mrs. Parsons. Murder is certainly not within the bounds of good service. They would never support anything improper."

Lady Pettifer chuckled. "I suppose murder to keep standards up would be too far a stretch."

"One would hope so. I'd probably be next in line otherwise."

The mirth melted from the lady's face. "I think we will all be surprised when it comes out," Lady Pettifer continued after a moment of silence. "If it comes out. Can you imagine if no one is ever caught and we are stuck here in perpetuity knowing someone around us had gotten away with murder." The woman shuddered. "You better leave me for a while now, Dory. I think I will rest."

"Of course," Dory said, putting the lady's gloves away in her armoire. Leaving, she closed the door behind her and walked downstairs. Gladys was already preparing for the evening meal, which was still hours away. "Lady Pettifer is napping," she said as she sat down heavily on one of the chairs. It had been a busy morning and afternoon. Lady Wallisford had had visitors, so between regular duties, lunch and afternoon tea, there hadn't been a moment to spare. Dory felt exhausted both in mind and body.

"Why don't you take a slice of the lemon drizzle cake left over from tea and go sit outside for a moment."

"Actually, that sounds heavenly." Dory rose and walked over to the serving tray still bearing leftovers and grabbed a slice, placing it on a paper napkin. Gladys was in charge of distributing any leftovers, so there were definitely some perks to having the cook as an aunt. "Thank you. I might take your advice and get a bit of sun."

Walking across the lawn with slice in hand, she made her way over to a large boulder which soaked up the sun all day long. It was a lovely place to sit on a sunny day. Hard, but warm and she could use some sun on her legs.

The drizzle cake was magnificent, soft and moist, with a tang of sweet lemon. If only she could cook and bake the way Gladys did. Unfortunately, it wasn't a gift that ran as readily on her side of the family. Dory's mother hadn't the inclination or skill to cook the way Gladys did.

Crumbs were left on the napkin and she crumpled it up and put it in her apron pocket. She also took off her white maid cap with the black ribbon running through it. It itched on her head sometimes, although most often she forgot it was there. Mrs. Parsons was not forgiving if she left her room without it.

The crunch of gravel drew her attention and she looked over to see DI Ridley walking along the path. "Miss Sparks," he said.

"Mr. Ridley. I didn't know you were here today."

"Just checking on some things." Leaping up on the boulder, he sat down next to her, looking more informal than she had ever seen him. He wore a blue suit today and stretched out his legs along the boulder. "This is a nice spot."

"When it's sunny," she said. "I hope everything is faring well with the investigation."

Taking a deep breath, he blew air out through puffed cheeks. "Some of the family members are making it difficult for me, feeling this should be done entirely without any inconvenience to them, or involve any participation from them. They are a disagreeable bunch."

He didn't know the half of it. They really did behave atrociously at times.

"They are always guarded when I'm around," he continued. "So are the servants, to be fair. Policemen make people uncomfortable."

"Oh, I heard something interesting the other day," Dory said. "I spoke to Michael Jones' brother."

"Stephen," DI Ridley cut in.

"Oh, you've spoken to him? Of course you have," she said, now feeling silly. "Well, he said that before she died, Nora had shown an interest in something Michael was working on. Some car, but he didn't know which or what, but that it was unusual that she was interested."

DI Ridley was quiet for a moment and Dory had no idea what he was thinking. He was so difficult to read. Deep in thought, he was stroking his hand across his chin as if feeling the stubble there. "I'm going to be releasing Michael Jones soon. The report is back on the bloody rag, which shows conclusively that it was the wrong blood type to be Nora Sands'. We have no evidence to hold him on at this point, which also means the true killer will know this now, too."

"That will please a lot of people."

"Pleasing people doesn't normally solve cases." Sitting up, he crossed his arms and leaned his elbows on his knees. "I must ask you a favor."

"Of course," Dory said. "How can I help?"

"I find that things are quite obscure for me within the house. People aren't saying what is really going on."

"Not sure I have noticed anything in particular going on, as such."

"But I would very much appreciate it if you would keep your eyes open, keep track of anything unusual."

"I'd be happy to," Dory said, feeling an immense sense of pride that he would ask her to help.

"Nothing more than that, just keep an eye on people coming and going."

Actually, that was a big task, because they came and went all the time, particularly Cedric, Vivian and Livinia. Livinia was the one that Dory knew the least about, and it seemed, according to everything Dory had heard, that Livinia had not been at home the night Nora died. Only Vivian, Lord and Lady Wallisford, and all of the staff. Probably the reason she hadn't given much thought to Livinia.

"I will," she finally said, thinking of the little notebook she had in her room and how she could use it to record information. "Livinia and Cedric were not in the house at the time."

"No, they are the only two people we can safely rule out. And as we don't have an exact time, we cannot take many of the alibis given amongst the staff as concrete either. But someone had motive, and access. To stab someone could take as little as seconds. They would only have to be gone from where they were supposed to be for a minute or two. Someone could actually slip out of a room and return before anyone noticed."

The task of solving this murder seemed insurmountable when put like that.

"And unfortunately," he continued, "there is no hint of a motive yet. Nothing out of the ordinary."

"Except that Nora was asking questions about some of Michael's work—what, we don't know. But Michael might remember."

"I will ask him," DI Ridley said and rose from the boulder.

"Am I a deputy now?" Dory asked with a smile.

"No," he said outright. "A mere informant."

"That does sound adventurous, doesn't it? A police informant."

"Don't get carried away. I am merely asking you to keep your eyes open when I am not here."

"Yes, sir," she said and saluted.

"We only really salute at funerals."

"Oh," Dory said and put her arm down. It just occurred to her that policemen sometimes died in the line of duty. It seemed a far-fetched idea from stories, but they probably did get fatally injured doing their job.

Chapter 16

Dory had no idea what she was supposed to do. Keep her eyes open and note who came and went, he had said—which was hard as she was often buried in a linen closet or down ironing something of Lady Pettifer's. Obviously, she paid most attention to Vivian, who, out of everyone, seemed the only one with some reason to kill Nora—even though he had emphatically denied having any kind of relationship with her. It wasn't inconceivable that some kind of assignation went on between them, even as she had a boyfriend. It was easy to see why someone would have their head turned by Vivian Fellingworth.

As for herself, Vivian showed absolutely no interest in her now that she'd shown she wasn't interested. It didn't surprise her. Men like him were after the easy conquests. They probably didn't even know how to do it otherwise.

But her focus on Vivian was because she had no idea why anyone else would kill her. And honestly, Vivian Fellingworth picked up and dropped girls on a regular basis. It was unlikely he would kill because of some over-amorous girl—that, he would know how to deal with.

It was hard to get any kind of grip on Nora. She had seemed so secretive. Gladys simply refused to speak of her, as if speaking of it would give breath to some evil in their midst.

If anyone knew her, it would be Mavis and Clara, and maybe Larry. But then, she didn't know that for sure. George the driver might know her better than assumed, and so could some of the gardening staff for all she knew.

George was sitting in the servants' dining hall, reading a paper. Out of all of them, excluding Mr. Holmes and Mrs. Parsons, he had the cushiest job—taking care of the car and driving when required. Beyond that, he had nothing to do and often sat around drinking coffee, smoking and reading the paper.

"Hello, George," Dory said and walked over to the sideboard to pour herself some hot water for tea. "How are you?"

"Oh, you know, steady as the wind," he said without looking up.

"It's a lovely day outside, isn't it?"

"I suppose."

Now Dory didn't know how to start the conversation she wanted to have. She cleared her throat and scratched her cap. "I hear they're releasing the mechanic that they suspected for Nora's murder."

"Oh, I hadn't heard."

"You must know him, being a mechanic."

"I suppose. He sees to the cars if there is something that needs replacing. Nice enough lad."

"Did you know Nora was seeing him?"

"Nope. She never told me, and neither did he."

"Was she interested in cars?"

"Nora?" he said with surprise. "Only in getting a lift."

"Did you give her lifts often?"

"If I came across her walking and I was alone. Only happened once in a blue moon." Dory supposed with family in the car, a walking Nora, or any other staff member, would just be driven past, left to take the long walk home. It had a logic Dory couldn't quite wrap her head around, but then the Fellingworth family, in general, had a logic she couldn't quite wrap her head around.

"No one seemed to know her well," Dory said.

He shrugged. "Some people are private people. In a place like this, it is all too easy to live in each other's pockets. Bit of distance makes for more cordial relationships, I find." Maybe that was why George was more aloof than others. He didn't tend to seek other people's company as much.

She had heard Mavis saying, however, that he had a sweetheart down in London and often went to see her when he could. That sounded about right; his heart never seemed to be here, instead gone out in the world somewhere— probably London.

"No one seemed to have a thing against her—still, she ended up murdered."

"I'm still thinking it was some lunatic wandering around, stumbling onto her and doing what madness drove him to."

"Yet no lunatic has been found."

"Probably moved on," he said, folding the paper and dropping it on the table. He walked out without another word.

Nothing, she had learned nothing from that conversation. Nora was as much a mystery as ever. It was almost easy to believe a lunatic had come in through the door and killed her, because no other motive was presenting itself. But there was no lunatic around. People had searched for one after the death, but no one was found anywhere nearby who didn't belong there.

Returning to her ironing, Dory finished and took the dress upstairs to hang. Lady Pettifer was not around, so Dory didn't stay; instead, she made her way downstairs.

"You there," a male voice said. It was the slow drawl of Lord Wallisford.

"Yes, my lord," Dory said and gave a curtsy. She had no idea if she was supposed to—she had never been directly addressed by him before. Now she blushed because she didn't know if she was acting like a ninny.

"I spilled something. Come help me clean it up."

"Of course," Dory said and made to follow when she realized she had absolutely nothing to clean with. She couldn't very well use her apron. "I'll grab the necessaries," she said and ran off. Running was probably not what she was supposed to do either, but she didn't stop until she got to the nearest closet and grabbed a pail and some rags.

In his study, there was tea spilled all over the Lordship's desk, and he held some dripping paper up over the desk.

"Damned thing," he said, referring to the tea cup. "Went down on the edge of a book. Completely ruined now, I suppose."

"Tea will stain the pages," Dory said. "I might try to save it, though, if you wish."

He grumbled, standing there in his green tweed jacket, still holding the document up. Dory placed her rag on the table and started to soak up the spilled tea. Taking the second rag, she patted the edge of the document he held in the air, careful not to smudge any ink. It had to be an important document if he sought to rescue it above everything else.

"You're the new girl," he said.

"Yes. I suppose I am here to replace Nora."

"Dreadful business."

"She seemed a nice girl. There is no hint of a reason why anyone killed her."

"I thought they arrested some boyfriend or other."

"He's been released after questioning," she informed him.

"Doesn't mean he's not guilty. Without proof, a person can't be held. Habeas corpus. Damned nuisance at times. It's usually the boyfriend, you know," he said as if he spoke with certainty. "Try to hide it afterwards. Passionate nature makes some do the queerest things."

"Do you know Michael Jones?"

"No, of course not. I am assuming that is the boyfriend."

"He works on some of your cars."

"Does he? George takes care of all that."

Dory smiled, twisting out the rag into the pail. "I'll get some water and wipe the desk, otherwise it will be sticky from the sugar."

"Ah, Holmes. A spill."

"I see," Mr. Holmes said curtly, having appeared at the door.

"I'll just get some water. Would you like me to hang the document up to dry?" Dory said, returning her attention to his lordship.

Lord Wallisford was still holding onto it. "Holmes, take care of this," he said, handing it over, making Dory feel overlooked and dismissed—deemed incapable of dealing with it.

Perhaps she shouldn't. Lord Wallisford trusted Mr. Holmes to dress him in the mornings, so it was natural he would turn to Mr. Holmes for assistance above anyone else. Otherwise, he thought her too big an idiot to deal with the care of a document—or distrusting her with its content.

They both walked out, leaving Dory to finish cleaning up.

The study was warm with the sun shining in through the window. She'd only been in here a couple of times cleaning the grate, but it was too warm for a fire now. On the desk still sat the book that had been inundated with tea and Dory picked it up. He hadn't answered if he wanted her to care for it, but she would try to recover the damage.

There wasn't much else on the desk, a pen made of onyx, an envelope holder and a telephone. The tea had gotten everywhere and she had cleaned up all she could see, but everything she lifted up had tea under it and it took a good half an hour to clean everything.

Well, she had learned two things. Lord Wallisford believed Michael Jones was guilty, and also, that unlike his sister, Lady Pettifer, he was wholeheartedly uninterested in the murder and the investigation. Unless he was a good actor—which somehow, Dory doubted.

Chapter 17

"A word," Mrs. Parsons said when Dory walked downstairs carrying the dirty plates after the family supper. The woman walked off to her small office and Dory rushed to the scullery to put down her burden.

She followed Mrs. Parsons to her office, who stood by the door as Dory walked in and closed it behind her. That was an ominous sign, Dory thought.

"Mr. Holmes spoke to me earlier," Mrs. Parsons said, smoothing her skirt as she sat down. "It seems you were in the study with Lord Wallisford earlier."

"Yes, he asked me to help him with some spilled tea."

"Mr. Holmes was under the impression you were questioning him."

Dory's mouth opened, but nothing came out, so she closed it again. Mrs. Parsons was still looking expectantly at her. "Well, I did inform him that Michael Jones had been released," Dory said quietly, knowing she was trying to make her actions sound more innocent than they were. She had been questioning him, or trying to.

"I understand that you perhaps hold some strange fascination with Miss Sands' demise, but it really isn't your place to indulge that fascination with Lord Wallisford— with any member of the family."

Dory was looking down on her lap, feeling her cheeks color. She was being admonished for her behavior. Although she wished to defend herself, she couldn't really. The accusation was true, and yes, it wasn't what she had been brought here for. "I'm sorry," she said.

Mrs. Parsons exhaled. "You don't seem to understand your place in the scheme of things."

There was no point mentioning that DI Ridley had asked her to keep an eye on things. Dory knew that would only upset Mrs. Parsons, who believed that for members of staff, their standards in providing service far outweighed in importance, any investigation the police were doing.

"I will be more mindful," Dory said after a moment of painful silence.

"See that you are. This is not an amusement park for you, Miss Sparks. This is your place of employment and there are standards of conduct you must uphold."

"I understand." Heat still flared up her cheeks. There was nothing Dory hated more than being told off, but there was no way to say her motives were honorable, because it wasn't her place to have honorable motives. She was here to clean and serve, and anything beyond that was not appreciated. And what policeman in their right mind would engage her to help, they would say.

"This is a warning to you," Mrs. Parsons said. "Any more transgressions on your part, then we will have to think long and hard if you belong in a place like this—in domestic service at all. It does not suit everyone, you know. You are only here because of Gladys, and she will be most dishonored if you can't figure out how to behave yourself."

Dory sat in silence until Mrs. Parsons dismissed her. Her cheeks still glowed by the time she walked out of the woman's office to take her seat for lunch. Gladys already sat at the table and by the look of it, none of this had been mentioned to her yet. Dory could imagine her scowl if she knew Dory had been accused of questioning members of the family about this murder. She would not be impressed and the scolding she got from Mrs. Parsons would be pressed on her again.

Lunch was an uncomfortable affair. Mrs. Parsons' accusations refused to leave Dory's mind. How could she be resented for trying to find out what happened to Nora? Shouldn't they all be trying to find out? But to tell her off, wasn't that careless?

She didn't dare look at anyone. The accusation had originally come from Mr. Holmes, who must have heard some of the discussion between her and Lord Wallisford. He and Mrs. Parsons would have reviewed her behavior between them, deemed it was inappropriate and decided she needed to be censured.

As soon as reasonable, she left the table, being too wound up to eat. She would suffer for that later, but right now, everything she put in her mouth went down like gravel. The need to escape the house was overwhelming and she made her way out into the sunshine, walking away and down to the pond. Partially, she wanted to be away, but she also felt the need to move.

Wind formed ripples across the water and three ducks swam lazily, safe from the lord of the manor's guns until autumn when the hunting season began. Strange how they were welcome friends now and mortal enemies once the hunting season started.

Dory sat down at the edge of the pond and pulled the heads off some daisies. The petals were soft between her fingers.

"You look troubled." A voice startled her when she hadn't been expecting anyone to be there. Dory turned to see Vivian.

"Where did you come from?" There was expanse of lawn all around and she hadn't seen him at all.

"You practically walked past me."

The acrid smoke from his cigarette came in wafts. He wore light brown slacks and a white shirt, looking very handsome and summery. As opposed to Cedric, Vivian embraced a level of informality at home. Cedric always stuck to his dark or tweed suits, having nowhere near the flair for style that Vivian did.

"Finding life at Wallisford Hall unbearable?" he said with a furrowed brow and a distant expression. "This place is terminally impuissant."

Pressing her lips together, she didn't want to admit that she had no idea what he meant. 'Impuissant' wasn't a word she knew and now she felt stupid. For all his shortcomings, he was educated, and with words like that, it showed.

"Just not sure domestic service is for me," she mumbled.

"Can't blame you. It must be tedious picking up after other people. I certainly wasn't made for it."

Not sure you were made for work in any capacity, she thought, but held her tongue. "Work is work, I suppose," she said. "Some of us must."

"Pity you, then," he said and squashed the butt of the cigarette on the lawn. He started to move away. Dory rose. As much as she was wary of Vivian, this was an opportunity to find out more. It seemed she wasn't entirely able to take her recent telling off to heart, or maybe she was spiting the censure given to her.

For all Vivian's blasé dismissal, he did seem to know what others did and thought.

"Do you know Michael Jones?" she asked before he'd moved too far away. He stopped and turned, his blond hair slightly catching in the breeze from the sun-bleached wave across his head. "Questioning me again?"

"I was just wondering. You seem to notice things." Flattery never hurt, she decided, and Vivian was probably susceptible to a bit of flattery. His eyebrows rose.

"Come to my room and I'll tell you everything I know about Michael Jones."

It was Dory's turn to frown. Like hell would she be talked into coming to his room. That look in his eye was part teasing and part something else she didn't want to explore. Yes, he was absolutely teasing her, knowing this made her uncomfortable—and he was using her curiosity against her. "That would be the day," she said with a snort, and he smiled.

"I don't know what it is you have against me. I'm almost hurt."

"Probably because you're *almost* hurt."

Twisting his head, he regarded her for a moment. "Yes, I know Michael Jones, he lives in the village. Not well, obviously. We've never been chums or anything. Too dense for my taste. Are you trying to impress that detective?"

"No!" she said, perhaps a little too forcefully.

"I think you're sweet on that detective." A playful smile spread across his lips. "How banal."

Dory was gritting her teeth. Oh, how she wanted to punch him in the face, but that would certainly get her fired. She was on thin ice as it was. Was this what he did—drove people up the wall? He certainly did his family members. Cedric was close to losing his composure every time Vivian was near.

"Why are you so caustic to everyone?" she accused.

"Because I can be," he said and walked away, lighting another cigarette. Dory watched him walking leisurely back to the house. People were simply toys to him—there for his amusement. By nature, he was callous, but callous enough to stab someone—that was on a whole deeper and darker layer of callousness. He was good at picking up on people's inner thoughts and emotions, but that made him observant rather than truly disregarding of other people's wellbeing. But then, it couldn't be said that he cared too much about offending anyone.

It had to be him, Dory said to herself. But it was impossible to see a motive. It certainly wouldn't be embarrassment, because he didn't care what people accused him of. That was not to say that blackmail wasn't a motive. Dory just wasn't sure Vivian would succumb. In fact, he would probably enjoy someone accusing him of something untoward—it fit with everyone's expectations of him. Would anyone really bat an eye if he were accused of sleeping with a servant girl? No, but the others would. Unfortunately, there was no evidence that Nora was seeing anyone but her boyfriend. In fact, sneaking around the house at night wouldn't happen for long under Mrs. Parsons watchful eye.

Chapter 18

"I'm so bored," Livinia said, lying back on Lady Pettifer's bed. She was dressed in jodhpurs and brown riding boots. "There is absolutely nothing to do here, and Father isn't letting me go back to London. I am absolutely wilting."

"Nonsense," Lady Pettifer said. "A bit of fresh air will serve your complexion, my dear. Where is that beau of yours?"

"You mean Patrick?"

That needed clarification, Dory thought as she stood to the side, brushing dog hair off Lady Pettifer's coat. She had been visiting a friend and had come back looking like she'd slept in a kennel at some point.

"Oh, I don't know," Livinia lamented. "We've had a falling out. He's so dull, I can't tell you."

"Well, then, it's good to be away for a while, builds a bit of mystery. Men do like a mystery."

An exasperated growl escaped Livinia, who was now staring up at the ceiling. "You are so old-fashioned."

"Men don't change, my dear. Fashions might, but men don't. Did you see that girl, Nora Sands, when you were last home?"

"The maid that got murdered?" Livinia sat up. Lady Pettifer gave Dory a small, conspiratorial wink. "I suppose so. I don't quite recall. Who notices such things? Particularly her; she was quiet like a mouse, wasn't she?"

"So she never spoke about her boyfriend?" Lady Pettifer said.

"Or anyone else she was seeing?" Dory added.

"Not to me. You think some jilted lover killed her? Not Nora. I couldn't imagine anyone looking twice at her. If there was anyone sure to die a virgin, it was her. Then again, there are some desperate people around."

"What makes you say that?" Dory asked.

"Who else are they going to turn to? The gardeners, for example. There aren't girls around for miles; they practically salivate whenever a girl is near." From what Dory had seen, that was an unjustified unkindness. Well, Larry was perhaps a little too keen for her to come to the movies with him.

"Did you see any of them speaking to Nora?" Lady Pettifer said.

"Why would I notice such things?" she said with a confused expression. "No, I never saw Nora speaking to the gardeners. Now, what is this blasted house party that we all have to be here for?" Livinia said. This was the first Dory had heard about a house party. It sounded like a mountain of work and no free time whatsoever, and Dory squashed the groan trying to escape her throat.

"Your mother has invited some of the notable parliamentarians around to try to help Cedric get himself more established. She expects you all to be on your best behavior."

"Stupid Cedric. Why do we all have to suffer because he's about to be buried in some dead-end committee? I don't see why he wanted to be a politician anyway. He couldn't charm a prostitute if his life depended on it."

"Livinia," Lady Pettifer said with exasperated disappointment. "We must all help, because it serves him and it serves the family. And it may well be that in the upcoming years, we all need to do our best to save the country."

Another groan escaped from Livinia and she flopped down on the bed again. "I am so tired of hearing about this bloody war that never seems to actually happen."

"Well, we are all praying that it doesn't," Lady Pettifer said, a sadness stealing into her voice. "There is nothing worse in the whole world than war."

Even Livinia picked up on her aunt's distress and rose from the bed, walking over to stroke Lady Pettifer along the shoulder. "I'm sure it won't come to that. To be safe, though. We should probably not push Cedric into politics, where cool minds are needed. He's annoying enough to send even the most sane person around the bend. Maybe they should send him over to deal with Hitler. He'll have that little imp crying into his sauerkraut."

Cheering up, Lady Pettifer chuckled. "You really are the sweetest person, Livinia, but I don't think we can leave you in charge of Cedric's advancement." Livinia rolled her eyes. "Or the country's," Lady Pettifer continued under her breath.

*

There was an anxious atmosphere that evening at supper. Livinia was still bored and stifled yawns throughout, Cedric was his usual reserved self, and Vivian was drunk—hardly to anyone's surprise. Lady Pettifer decided not to join them and retreated to her room with a headache.

"I haven't a thing to wear," Livinia lamented when they left the dining room and retreated into the parlor. "And why is it so cold tonight? This blasted house never warms up. We cannot do without a fire."

Dory felt Mr. Holmes' eyes on her and she turned from where she placed the large serving tray down to see that yes indeed, he was placing the task of lighting the fire with her. It was the middle of summer, but still, a fire was needed. It wasn't even cold, but then Livinia did insist on wearing those light chiffon dresses. Granted, it was a stunning dress in light green material, but it couldn't be more than wearing a cloud floating around her body.

"Wallis Simpson's wedding dress looks white in the photos, don't you think?" Livinia said to her mother as Dory walked in the room with a wood carrier to crouch down by the fireplace. "It was light blue, apparently. So stunning. No one can argue that she is the only one in that royal household with any sense of style. She would have made a fantastic queen. Married in Paris. It sounds so romantic." On this, Dory and Livinia were in complete agreement.

"If you call giving up your crown romantic," Cedric said with a snort.

"He is a singularly stupid man. If she cared at all about him, she would have kept the status quo and remained as his mistress," Lady Wallisford said. "Goes to show how ambitious that woman is. But it didn't work, did it? She gambled and now she's lost, stripped of royal title and all the royal privileges."

"She's still a duchess," Livinia said.

"Duchess of what? A lost throne? As much use as a toilet. Well, I hope she's happy. She just about ripped this country apart with her ambition."

"Not all the evils in the world are caused by Mrs. Simpson," Vivian said.

"We should have the means of getting rid of people like that. Coming over here and upsetting everything, refusing to understand their own position." Lady Wallisford was getting very passionate about her opinion.

"God help us all if we don't conform to our positions," Vivian said with a surprising amount of spite.

"If Edward was king, why couldn't he just tell them that he was marrying her and they should just suck it up."

"Because it was never about Wallis fucking Simpson," Vivian stated.

"Apologize this minute," Livinia demanded. "You're a disgusting cur and you have absolutely no idea what you're talking about."

Also surprising was Livinia's degree of anger, thought Dory as she lit the kindling she had stacked around in a wooden triangle.

Lord Wallisford sat buried behind his evening paper and ignored the discussion around him.

"Both of you," Lady Wallisford said. "I won't forgive either of you if you behave like this when our guests come. You will be on your best behavior, or father will have to cut your weekly allowance."

"Of course, Mother," Vivian said, putting on his most charming voice. "We will all do our very best to fix the hash job Cedric has made of his career."

"Don't be tiresome, Vivian," Lady Wallisford said with exasperation. "It will be a very dull summer for you if you upset me in this. Your brother's career is important and you will do nothing to spoil it."

"Why? He's going to inherit the whole estate. It's not like he needs a career."

"As opposed to you," Livinia said sweetly. "You're the one who actually needs a career, or are you going to live under your brother's roof for the rest of your life?"

"Unfortunately, she is right, Vivian. You really need to turn your attention to your future. You'll either have a role in men's society or you'll become an add-on in the women's."

Vivian rose and stepped over to the bar to pour himself another drink. Anger practically dripped off him. That was harsh, even in Dory's book. This family seemed always to be at each other's throats, ripping each other apart with insults. It was like nothing she had ever known. Her family supported her in everything, even when she made a complete mess of something. "Never mind, lamb," her mother would say. "It's a new day tomorrow."

"Are you too incompetent to light a fire?" Vivian said harshly, standing with his back to her.

"Yes, I am," she said, "but never mind, it's a new day tomorrow."

"Oik wisdom?" He turned to her and took a sip of his large whiskey, practically standing over her as she crouched by the fire.

Dory grit her teeth and smiled. "I am so glad I am missing my supper for this."

The viciousness on his face softened slightly. "Are you wondering why Mrs. Simpson would go anywhere near British refined society?"

"I'm actually paid to not wonder about anything when it comes to British refined society. It is a necessary quality for anyone having to deal with you." Grabbing the empty wood carrier, she left out of the small servants' doorway that led to the landing off the staircase heading downstairs. Right now, she didn't care about how vulgar and nasty the Fellingworths were to each other. Her supper was getting cold and that was more important to her than any of Vivian Fellingworth's insults. They would burn if she let them, so she refused to entertain them at all. He was nothing but a little boy fighting with his sister and backing down because his allowance was about to be cut. He could call her oik as much as he wanted. It really was understandable why people ripped into him. He seemed to goad everyone around him into viciousness. Or they all fed off each other. She didn't care which.

Chapter 19

Today it rained without stop. The skies were an endless blanket of gray and the air was cold and moist. Even being summer, it had a chill, and a certain restlessness had descended over the house. Tempers and pleasantries were short and Dory didn't mind losing herself in some mundane work.

Both Cedric and Vivian were gone, seeking diversion and entertainment elsewhere. Dory wished she could be away from the house for a while as well. Working here, her life felt small. Seeing the same faces every day; never anything new. It was dull. Even Lady Pettifer found it dull.

Dory had been given the task of cleaning the water closet with its white tiles with grout that needed scrubbing, so she was down on her knees with a toothbrush, listening to the rhythmic patter of rain on the foggy window.

It wasn't just the weather that was a source of frustration. DI Ridley had been in the house, speaking to Mr. Holmes and she could sense his frustration from a distance. It wouldn't surprise her one bit if people were actively hampering his investigation by simple disinterest. Nora Sands was a part of this household. Didn't they care that something awful had happened to her?

She knew exactly what they would say. Of course they cared, but what could they do? It couldn't be that anyone here was responsible. But there had to be. There just didn't seem a way to getting to the truth. Everyone left it to the police to deal with, not seeing that they should have to play a role—or be inconvenienced by this.

As far as she knew, there had been no progress— not that DI Ridley kept her abreast of the developments, but the gossip around here tended to convey everything. Everyone was interested in the investigation—as long as it didn't include them.

With frustration, Dory dropped the toothbrush and sat back on her haunches. Her knees and back ached from scrubbing and she needed to stretch. It was work well done. She could clearly see where she had worked and where she hadn't. Finishing was going to take ages.

A quick knock on the door drew her attention. Someone must want to use the lavatory. "Just a minute," she said and gathered up her brushes and the tub of grout cleaner.

The door opened. "Dory, Lady Wallisford has asked to see you," Clara said.

"What?" Dory said with surprise. This couldn't be good.

"She's in the parlor having afternoon tea. What have you done?"

"I didn't do anything," Dory said impotently. The look in Clara's eyes said she was unconvinced. Dory should have known Mrs. Parsons would not have been the end of it. Maybe now she was going to be fired and by the end of the day would be dragging her suitcase out into the rain as they threw her out. Maybe Larry would be merciful and drive her to the train station. Did she have enough money for the fare? She tried to remember how much she'd spent.

Dory sighed and made her way out of the water closet, putting her cleaning materials away in the nearest closet. A smudge marred her apron and she wondered if she should run upstairs and change it. Adding that little bit of extra proof that this job was beyond her hurt her pride, so she ran as fast as she could. If she was going to be fired, she wanted to look presentable—not as if their decision was entirely justified.

A clean apron tied around her waist, she made her way to the parlor behind a large, white door. She knocked carefully, almost imperceptibly. Mrs. Parsons opened, looking stern and disapproving. Dory should have known she would dob her in, the traitor. But then, Mrs. Parsons would never take her side over the lady of the house—no matter what.

Lady Wallisford was sitting on a sofa, with Livinia on the other and Lady Pettifer in a chair. A tea service had been placed in front of them and half-drunk cups of tea sat unattended.

What hurt most was that Lady Pettifer was there. Dory had believed they had reached an understanding, a friendship even—hence, Dory had been less reserved than it turns out she should have been. Perhaps there was no trusting these people.

"Miss Sparks," Lady Wallisford said, her neck tall and regal, managing to look down her nose at Dory from a sitting position. That was quite a feat, Dory had to admit.

"There have been some disturbing noises about you and I thought we would take this opportunity to clear things up."

Dory looked over at Mrs. Parsons, whose hands were clasped together. She wasn't looking Dory in the eyes. Then she looked at Lady Pettifer, who looked slightly confused, listening intently. Maybe she wasn't a part of this and didn't know what was about to be said. Dory hoped so, even if it served her no good whatsoever. It would gladden her to know her judgment of Lady Pettifer's character hadn't been completely off—or that you categorically couldn't trust people in her position. It would hurt to know that station went against things like confidence and trust.

"I understand," Lady Wallisford continued, "that you have been interrogating all and sundry about the unfortunate events prior. As you can imagine, we wish to live here in peace and tranquility, and not be accosted by staff interrogating for their own amusement."

Lady Wallisford looked at her expectantly and Dory burned with embarrassment, and also offense for Nora. "I was just trying to understand Nora Sands better." Dory was mumbling, her cheeks burning red.

"Do you fancy yourself a detective, do you? Is it a role you feel you can fulfill better than the police?" Lady Wallisford chuckled. "Did she not question you, Livinia?"

"Yes, she did," Livinia stated, casting a glance over to Dory.

"And you, Constance?" she said, turning to Lady Pettifer.

Lady Pettifer blinked repeatedly. "Well, naturally we have spoken about it at length."

Raising her eyebrows further, Lady Wallisford looked as if her point had been reinforced.

"I had, of course, asked her to make some inquiries," Lady Pettifer continued. "How else are we going to find out who killed that poor girl. Dory, here, was acting on my mandate."

Thunderclouds broke through Lady Wallisford's expression. "That is hardly her place. And it is hardly your responsibility. It is the police's. We can't be running around second guessing their activities."

"We're not second-guessing, Honoria. No one is giving that poor detective the time of day. How is he supposed to solve this crime if no one is answering his questions?"

"Who isn't answering his questions? We've answered every question he's put to us. I would thank you not to use my servants to play silly games."

An uncomfortable silence settled between the ladies, like two bulls in a paddock eyeing each other up.

Technically, Lady Pettifer hadn't asked her to question people, but Dory was elated that she hadn't been wrong to trust the woman, that they had reached a common ground on which a sort of friendship had been achieved. And that the woman had her back when things got sticky. It was quite something.

"I can't have her running around interrogating people. It's unseemly."

"To whom?"

"She's a servant, and not a terribly good one at that. I have to let her go," Lady Wallisford said. Livinia was examining her nails, completely uninterested.

"Then I will retain her." Charged silence settled. "She does an admirable job for me and if I ask her to do some inquiries, she does an admirable job at that as well."

"Sometimes I wonder if you have completely lost your marbles," Lady Wallisford griped dismissively and Dory could see Lady Pettifer bristle with offense. "Aldus always thought you pottering around that big house in France would test your faculties."

"I assure you, Honoria, dear, my faculties are perfectly fine," Lady Pettifer said tightly, her voice sharp and crisp. "Dory, why don't you go see to my evening dress. It might need an airing."

"Yes, my lady," Dory said with a curtsy, not daring to look up.

Mrs. Parsons opened the door and Dory walked out. So, she'd just lost one job and gained another as Lady Pettifer's maid. If this was a real job, she didn't know, but it sure saved her pride if nothing else.

Closing the door, Mrs. Parsons looked at her sharply. Dory didn't report to her anymore. "I suppose you will be staying with us for however long Lady Pettifer does, or how long *she* determines you suitable." There was a nasty edge to her voice. Obviously, Mrs. Parsons had wanted her fired as well, had probably expected to send her packing. For all Dory knew, her belongings might already be packed upstairs.

"I only managed to clean part of the bathroom grout," Dory said with her head held high. That was no longer her job and Mrs. Parsons would have to find someone else to finish it. Dory no longer took orders from Mrs. Parsons. As Lady Pettifer's lady's maid, none of those household chores were hers anymore. Her concern was now exclusively Lady Pettifer.

Chapter 20

Becoming Lady Pettifer's maid meant a vast decrease in Dory's workload. All she had to do now was take care of Lady Pettifer and her things, but when she'd seen to those things, there wasn't much for her to do.

She had learned not to spend that free time down in the servants' area, as her idle hours built resentments with everyone else. Their disapproval was quite clear; they didn't approve of her switching her alliances to Lady Pettifer, even though she had no choice in the matter. Mrs. Parsons was particularly cold, refusing to say anything to Dory. She was now treated as a guest, a visiting servant. She was given her meals and the use of the amenities of the house, but she was no longer part of the household.

Clara and Mavis were not quite as cold, but they were much more guarded around her now than they used to be, taking their cues from Mrs. Parsons and Mr. Holmes. Gladys was still kind, of course, but she was also aware of what had happened. Family ties were not as easy to put aside. She tried to console Dory, not that Dory needed consoling as she was quite happy in her new role. Although how long it would last, she wasn't sure.

While she had served as Lady Pettiford's maid since her arrival, the woman hadn't intended on taking on a maid. Dory didn't know if she could actually afford to do so, or whether this was just an act of pride, countermanding Lady

Wallisford, who had so insulted Lady Pettifer the previous day.

"No matter," Gladys said, kneading dough on the large, wooden workbench. "Obviously, Lady Pettiford will only be here for a few short months. When she goes, you likely have to find a new job somewhere else."

"I realize this," Dory said.

"The upside, I suppose, is that Lady Pettifer seems to like you, so there's a good chance you'll get a reference. Without a reference, you will never get another job."

Dory wasn't sure she could mention to her aunt that she wasn't sure domestic service was for her. She didn't love working here; she found it droll. Then again, working in an office hadn't worked out that well for her, either. The reference hadn't been particularly good; the one Lady Pettiford would give her would probably be better. Still, Dory wasn't sure that this lifestyle was for her. Not that she felt comfortable telling Gladys this, who had spent all her life in domestic service and seemed quite comfortable in a house like this.

"It will all work out," Gladys said, trying to be reassuring. "You have a few months to think about it, before you have to act. Try not to think about it now. Summer is here and for the next few months, you seem to have it easy." Gladys patted her hand, leaving an impression of flour.

Dory would agree, if it wasn't for how uncomfortable she felt around the others. She was not quite appreciated the way she had been, although saying that, she hadn't really been all that appreciated before either. Her curiosity had gotten her into strife again, which it always seemed to do.

"Take a bun," Gladys said, pushing the baking basket over to Dory and she gratefully took one of the Chelsea buns that were still warm to the touch.

"Thank you, Aunt," she said with a smile. "You're the best." With a smile, Dory left her to find something to occupy herself. She'd tried to offer her services to help, but Gladys wouldn't have it. There was pride in such things, Dory had learned. Suggestions she wasn't coping were a profound insult, even though Dory had simply been trying to help.

She walked out into the sunshine, intent on getting some fresh air. There were still puddles of water around, but the sun had returned. A nicely warm breeze floated across the land, shivering the trees in the distance. The leaves sang whenever the wind picked up.

The bun was sweet and sticky and Dory enjoyed it immensely. As she wandered away from the house to the farm outbuildings, she came across George polishing a car. Being warm, he'd taken his jacket off and was working in his shirtsleeves.

"Dory," he said with a nod, acknowledging her. She cleared the last of the sticky bun off her fingers and wiped them on her dress.

"Hello, George. Lovely weather we have today."

"Yes," he replied. "I hear there have been some developments at the house concerning you."

"It seems I have shifted allegiances and am now Lady Pettifer's maid."

"So I heard." He was polishing something metal in his hand with a rag. "Does this mean that you follow her back to France?"

"I shouldn't think so," Dory said. She hadn't even thought about it. Would Lady Pettifer take her back to France? Wouldn't that be something? She had never left England, so going all the way to France would be an adventure beyond anything she'd actually contemplated.

"I understand that Lady Pettifer has the maids she needs in France already."

George nodded, still busy polishing whatever he was holding in his hand. Dory didn't know cars all that well and had no idea what part he held in his hand. "Funny thing," he said. "After we spoke last time, I thought about when I saw Nora Sands last. It took some thinking, but I believe I saw her last up on the Common Road."

"The Common Road? Is that close by?"

"It's not too far away, but is a strange place for her to be. I thought so at the time. It doesn't lead to anything in particular and she was on her bicycle. I didn't see her again after that. Obviously, she did return at some point. I'm sure it doesn't mean anything, but that was the last time I saw her."

"You have no idea what she would be doing on the Common Road?"

George shrugged. "None whatsoever. Like I said, doesn't lead anywhere in particular, at least nowhere close enough she should bicycle to. Maybe she just wanted some exercise."

"Was she known for taking exercise, for taking the bicycle out?"

"She would take it to the village on occasion," he said, smiling as he started rubbing the bonnet of the car again. The olive green of the machine gleamed, as did all the chrome surrounding it. It was a beautiful machine, even she knew that.

Giving George a wave, she kept on walking over to the copse of trees across the parkland at the west side of the house. She'd never heard anything of Nora going for a bicycle ride shortly before her death. Where would she be going? What was she doing out on the Common Road? It certainly wasn't on the way to Quainton, or to Aylesbury. What was she doing there? No one had mentioned this before.

Obviously, she wasn't murdered out there, because she had been seen afterward by other people. Was she meeting someone? Was that person responsible for what happened to her later? There were still unknown aspects of Nora's life, and what she was doing. DI Ridley had never mentioned any of this, and Dory didn't know if he even knew George had seen her there.

Dory felt in her gut that this was important. Any way you cut it, it was unusual behavior. Nora must have been doing something, something away from the house. This could actually be very relevant. In fact, she needed to tell DI Ridley about this. Perhaps she should go upstairs and talk to Lady Pettifer about it.

Maybe she could send a note, but a part of her almost wanted to tell him in person. He was a curious man and Dory's curiosity about him had only grown. She hadn't seen him around the house for a few days, and now she was wondering what he was off doing—if he had learnt anything interesting.

What she knew for sure, though, was that she needed to tell him about this, about what she'd just heard. It had to be important.

Chapter 21

Again, Dory found herself cycling to Quainton. Having talked over what she'd learnt with Lady Pettifer, they both agreed that there was something queer about Nora Sands being out on the Common Road, which incidentally wasn't actually named the Common Road, but that was what everyone around here called it. Way back, apparently it had been called the Common Road when it was used commonly to herd cattle southwards, or so Lady Pettifer had told her—a fact Dory didn't feel she actually needed.

Lady Pettifer did sometimes explain obscure facts and details about the house and surrounding district. Dory had gotten used to receiving such inconsequential details; it was part of being Lady Pettifer's maid.

Most of the water from the recent rains had drained away and the puddles along the gravel road were all dry, leaving pockmarks along the stretch of the road. Technically, Dory was on another of her sherbet gathering missions, if anyone asked. Both Dory and Lady Pettifer's interest in this investigation had become a contentious topic in the house, not that Lady Pettifer was about to be swayed from her curiosity, or perceived duty to do all she could. Dory admired that about her.

Unfortunately, DI Ridley was nowhere to be seen, nor was he in the small constabulary office, or the pub.

Dory ended up sitting on one of the stone walls with a pocket full of sherbets, not knowing what to do. Eventually, a dark blue car came driving down the street and parked in front of the constabulary. She could see it was him through the car window and he glanced at her without any further acknowledgment.

"Am I right in assuming you are waiting for me?" he said when he got out and closed the door.

"I suppose I am," she said, jumping off the wall. "I heard something interesting that I thought you should perhaps know about—we thought you should know about," she corrected herself.

"Who is *we*?"

"Myself and Lady Pettifer." Dory thought it best not to mention that she had actually been fired for asking too many questions, as he had only told her to observe. Well, she had done a little more and had learned about Nora being somewhere no one could explain because of it.

"Well, you'd better come to the pub, then," he said, already walking in that direction. Dory followed him into the rather deserted pub where only a few elderly patrons sat. It was a little past the lunchtime rush. "A pint," he said to the barman, before turning to her. "What can I get you?"

"Just a lemon barley for me," Dory said with a smile, wondering what the barman thought this meeting was. It wasn't the first time she was seen in the pub with DI Ridley. Could be the man presumed there was more than a strictly professional relationship between them. That couldn't be further from the truth. All the same, it made her blush. She couldn't even imagine what it would be like to be asked to the pub by someone like him for any such reasons.

Dory stepped back as he paid for the drinks and carried them over to a small table at the far end of the pub. That only made it seem more like a secret assignation, but she understood that privacy was an important issue for someone like him.

"So what is it you came all this way to tell me? You could have phoned."

"Lady Pettifer wanted some sherbets and the phones are heavily monitored at the Hall."

"Is that a problem?" he asked with a raised eyebrow.

"Well, it is if someone really doesn't want Nora's killer to be discovered."

"What makes you say that?" It was he that was interrogating her now. His eyes were piercing, as if he watched every expression she made. It was quite disconcerting.

Dory didn't really want to get into the whole kafuffle about the accusations against her for playing detective. "It is only logical, isn't it?" She couldn't manage to look him in the eye. He would see the lie—she was sure of it. "Anyway, I was speaking to George Henry, Lord Wallisford's chauffeur, and he mentioned that the last time he'd seen Nora Sands, she was bicycling out on the Common Road. He thought it was queer because there was no reason she should be there, and it leads to nowhere she would particularly want to go."

DI Ridley twisted his head and looked distracted, as though he was turning this new information over in his head. He bit his lip, which drew Dory's attention and distracted her. "He didn't mention it when I spoke to him."

"Probably didn't think of it. But what was she doing there?"

"I have no idea," Ridley said. "There is really nothing out that way?"

"Not for miles, or so I've heard. I don't really know the area well. Maybe she was meeting someone?"

"Maybe," Ridley said absently. He took a swig of his pint and remained silent.

"Lord Wallisford still thinks Michael Jones is responsible because he was her boyfriend. And Livinia Fellingworth couldn't be less interested in who killed her." Cedric was someone she hadn't talked to, but his alibi for the time of the murder had been confirmed. For a moment, she wondered if she should mention Vivian Fellingworth and their discussion where he'd more or less propositioned her to come to his room. "I don't think either of them know Michael Jones, but Vivian Fellingworth and George Henry both do."

"They both deal with cars, so that is logical. So no one has been able to establish why Nora was out on the Common Road?"

"I take it Michael Jones didn't mention anything related to it."

"No," Ridley said and brought out his cigarette case, taking one out and tapping the end on the case. He offered the case to her, but she shook her head. Lighting the cigarette, he inhaled and blew the smoke out. "We need to find out why she was on that road." His attention was on her now.

"They aren't going to talk to me about it, some of them," she finally had to admit, because quite a few of the people there would clam up if she even mentioned Nora at this point.

"I suppose I need to make another visit to the house, then," he said and Dory could well imagine how excited Lady Wallisford would be about it.

"There is a weekend party coming up. Political friends of Lord Wallisford. They are trying to establish Cedric in Parliament. Lady Wallisford would see it as a wildly inappropriate time."

"Is that right? Well, unfortunately, we do not plan murder investigations around the gentry's social calendars." The bored expression on his face said he didn't worry about Lady Wallisford's disapproval, or maybe he didn't like the woman that much. Who could blame him—she was awful.

Ridley looked away and out of the window. Dory watched him, having a moment doing so when she wasn't observed. His pint was half finished now and she hadn't even touched her lemon barley yet. She took a deep gulp of the both sweet and tart liquid.

"I can give you a ride to the hall," he said, looking back at her and flicking ash into the ashtray.

"You're going right now?"

"No point waiting."

"I have a bicycle, so I need to bring it back, but thank you for the offer." It was probably best anyway. It was hard to predict how it would be perceived if she came back in his company. They were suspicious of her as it was, which was a problem in terms of how useful she could be. It seemed she had burned her bridges with the people at the house. Except Lady Pettifer—and maybe Vivian, who had yet again flirted with her. More than flirted—he'd practically propositioned her.

Drawing a deep breath, Dory sighed. Something still felt really off with Vivian. There was something there and she couldn't put her finger on it. He had no alibi for the time of the murder, but there was nothing linking him to Nora, other than his propensity to get involved with the maids—a habit he had given up on long ago, according to his own telling—while at the same time inviting her to his room for not altogether innocent reasons, she was sure.

"No time like the present," Ridley said when she finished her lemon barley and he stood. "Safe ride back." Dory smiled at him, feeling tickled that he cared about her safety. For being an actual gentleman, Vivian Fellingworth cared much less than DI Ridley. But then, with his callow and blasé behavior, she couldn't see him as half the man DI Ridley was. The thought of how offended Vivian would be if he knew she thought so made Dory smile. He acted like he owned the world and everything he touched turned to gold, but his position, good looks and fortune didn't make true substance. It took something other than that—something quiet and resolute, something strong.

Chapter 22

The house, at least the servants' area, turned into utter chaos as the weekend's visitors arrived. This was a completely different gathering of people than the previous parties at the hall. Firstly, they were mostly men, the timbre of murmur in the parlor much lower. Some women accompanied their husbands, but this was definitely a male-centric event.

Vivian was in his element, standing confidently with his hand in his pocket, dressed quite informally in cream slacks and a knitted vest. As Dory brought in a bucket of ice, she heard his laughter from amongst the group of men. For all his intermittent boorish behavior, he did so easily slip into any social setting. Cedric was more awkward, more formally dressed and stood by his father. Perhaps it was a shame that Vivian didn't have the ambition to enter politics, but then he didn't seem to have ambition of any kind.

To her distress, Vivian was walking over to the side table where Dory was depositing ice and tidying glasses and decanters. Mr. Holmes stood by, carefully watching with his eagle eyes. The house's need for help was so dire, they had no choice but to accept the assistance she offered. Dory hoped that would go some way to mending fences with her technically former colleagues. She wasn't one to thrive on discord.

Vivian poured a large glass of whiskey for himself. "I'm going to need this to get through the afternoon in this crowd," Vivian said dolefully. "The stalwart belief in inherent superiority is practically dripping on the floor."

"I thought inherent superiority would be something you would loyally subscribe to," she said, unable to help herself, while at the same time glancing over to see if Mr. Holmes was observing her. His attention seemed to be on his lordship.

Vivian made the sound of a cat's growl and smiled wickedly. "Careful, Miss Sparks, your working-class resentment is showing through."

Now Dory really did feel like punching him, but she calmed herself. "Pointing out your foibles is hardly resentment, simply an observation."

"Is there a problem?" Mr. Holmes said, appearing next to Dory. How had he moved so quickly?

"Oh, go away Holmes. I don't need you to work my mouth for me."

Mr. Holmes had no choice but to walk away when ordered and Dory burned with embarrassment. "Thank you so much. My position here is hard enough without you making it worse."

Lifting an olive to his mouth, he pulled the wooden spear out and bit—not unlike what he was doing to her relationship with the other staff. That was the thing with Vivian Fellingworth, he didn't care about the consequences to other people from his actions. It was all about him. "I wasn't aware your position was hard."

"Didn't you hear? I was fired."

"Then why are you still here?"

"Because your aunt hired me again. Now, go away." She would literally push him away if she couldn't feel Mr. Holmes attention burning into her back. Grabbing an empty decanter of cognac, she walked out of the room before Vivian had the opportunity to sully her standing further.

Clara was downstairs, ironing a tuxedo and Dory headed straight for her. "Are you sure Vivian Fellingworth wasn't giving Nora a hard time?"

"What do you mean?" Clara said, letting the iron rest on the heating plate.

"Teasing, prodding, generally making a nuisance of himself."

"Is that what he's doing to you?"

Was there a point in denying it? "Yes."

Clara pursed her lips for a moment as if contemplating something. "Not that I ever saw. Shortly before... you know, Nora's unfortunate demise, I saw no interest in her coming from him. Truthfully, he wasn't around a lot and before that, there was a married woman he was flirting with around Christmas time."

Dory rolled her eyes. Of course he would flirt with a married woman. "From around here?"

"No, she was up from London. I don't recall seeing her before. She was slightly older, and she and Vivian... well, you got the feeling they knew each other more intimately. Just little touches here and there. Nothing overt. But I saw nothing between him and Nora. And she disappeared every spare moment."

"Did you hear that George saw her cycling up on the Common Road?"

"He might have mentioned it."

"What was she doing up there?"

Clara shrugged. "Haven't a clue."

"She was going somewhere, but to where?"

"Maybe she was meeting Michael?" Clara added.

"No, I don't think so. In fact, he didn't even seem to know about it at all."

"She must have been meeting someone."

Vivian? Dory asked in her mind. Was there some cottage up that way?

"Miss Sparks," Mr. Holmes deep voice sounded from the doorway. Wonderful, she had been caught questioning again. "A word."

With an internal wince, she followed him out into the hall.

"About your relationship with certain members of the family," he started.

"I have no relationship with anyone other than Lady Pettifer," Dory cut in, unable to hold back her frustration. "Vivian Fellingworth has set himself on teasing me. I have not invited it or asked for it in any way."

Mr. Holmes considered her with hard eyes. "It is inappropriate."

"I completely understand," she said. "But I have very little influence with him. If you find some way of telling him to stop, I would be much obliged."

"Probably best to stay clear," he said with a sniff. "It is unseemly him spending any part of a gathering conversing with a member of the staff." Why was he telling her this? What was she supposed to do about it? Dory was losing her patience. Patience was a virtue, but it was one she hadn't readily mastered.

"And how would you like me to deal with it when he does? Should I run away? Refuse to answer his questions?"

"No, of course not. Just act with some decorum."

Gritting her teeth together, she tried to smile. Decorum? How had she ever not acted with decorum?

Mr. Holmes gave her a pointed look to accentuate his point and Dory fought her mounting frustration as he turned to walk away.

"Mr. Holmes," she said with a nod. With a growling exhale, Dory turned to be surprised by a figure in the doorway. DI Ridley, standing there as though he'd just observed the whole exchange.

"And what type of questions are Vivian Fellingworth putting to you?" The expression on his face was indeterminable again, the way it was when he interrogated. Dory blushed, unable to bring herself to state that he'd asked her to join him in his room, or offered her leisurely rides in his car.

"He has just developed a habit of teasing me," Dory said and Ridley remained quiet that way he did, as if driving people to speak further. She refused. "No one I've spoken to knows why Nora was on the Common Road."

"No, same for me."

"It's a shame she didn't have a diary where she wrote all her thoughts down. That would make everything so much easier. Perhaps everyone should keep a diary, just in case."

"She didn't. I checked with her family and there was no diary with her effects."

"So there are two things we don't know—things she was doing or interested in, including what interested her with Michael's work, and what she was doing on the Common Road."

"Well, according to Michael Jones, she had asked about the work he'd done on one of the Wallisford estate cars," Ridley said. "He hadn't seen it as unusual at the time, her being curious about the work he did for the estate."

"Which was?"

"Nothing major. Some scratches on the paint."

"Scratches on paint," Dory repeated, her mind trying to make some sense of this. George and his incessant polishing came to mind. "Oh." She was disappointed, having hoped this would result in something more extraordinary.

"Not the first time one of the cars had been scratched up, either, according to Mr. Jones," Ridley continued. Blimey, scratching one of those cars must have been a firing offense for George. He must live in terror of scratching one of those fancy cars.

Taking his cigarette case out, he brought one out and tapped it before giving her a nod. He was going outside and Dory watched him for a moment, still trying to make sense of everything he'd departed. Well, that was one mystery that didn't seem to lead to any spectacular revelations.

Dory continued into the staff dining room, where she found George sitting with the paper. In all the rush of the house, he had nothing to do. No one was going anywhere and all the guests' cars were bedded down for the night.

"I heard you scratched one of the lordship's cars a few months back," she said. "That must be devastating."

"Not me," he said, standing up and putting his jacket on. "I never hurt any of my babies."

"So there were no scratches?"

"Oh, there were some scratches alright, we had to repaint the whole panel, but I wasn't to blame. What do you take me for, an amateur?" Taking a last gulp of his coffee, he made to leave.

"Then who scratched it?"

"Not sure," he said with a shrug. "Had to be one of the family. No one else would drive those cars other than me. No one owned up, though."

"Did Nora know how to drive?"

"Not to save her life. Tell you the truth, she wasn't all that proficient on a bicycle either."

Chapter 23

The salon was deserted when Dory went upstairs again. Glasses were strewn on every surface and Dory started collecting them. Mr. Holmes was nowhere to be seen now, having gone wherever the lordship needed him to be, which was out on the lawn, judging by the sound of guns firing.

Over at the window, she saw the group outside, a few with cracked open guns resting on the crooks of elbows. They hadn't gone far, and were standing on the edge of the elevated section of the lawn. Others still had drinks, like Vivian did. He smoked a cigar, watching as the clay birds whizzed in the air, and the shooter missed. "Bird away," someone yelled.

Dory resumed collecting glasses, and when finished, she made her way upstairs to Lady Pettifer's room. "All that shooting is getting on my nerves," she said when Dory arrived. "They do seem to be enjoying themselves. When I was young, it wasn't uncommon that they would release actual pigeons to shoot."

"How grisly," Dory said with a grimace.

"It was, rather. Made an unbelievable mess. Poor birds. Creatures shouldn't die for the entertainment of others."

Dory couldn't help Nora entering her mind. She hoped Nora hadn't died for something so callous. Surely, no one could be that callous. There was evil in the world, but Dory had never really seen any. Sure, there were stupid people doing stupid things—petty things—but she had never really seen true cruelty and sheer disinterested callousness.

"How is Cedric doing?" Lady Pettifer asked, sitting at her dressing table.

Walking over to the window, Dory looked out, seeing him again standing next to his father. He had a gun resting over his arm. "It appears he has been shooting."

"Good," Lady Pettifer said. "He doesn't have the force of personality that Vivian does. But that is usually the way with eldest brothers. They are serious and composed, while the younger who doesn't carry the mantle of responsibility and tradition tend to flourish in different ways."

'Flourish' might not be the word Dory would use for Vivian Fellingworth, but the viewpoint of a loving aunt was very different. To a loving aunt, he was a mischievous scoundrel. Lady Pettifer seemed to actually enjoy his antics. Maybe because they were rarely aimed at her. They seemed to have a special relationship where he toned down his caustic nature. Lady Pettifer would be destroyed if it turned out that Vivian was responsible for something truly nefarious.

The sun gleamed in his blond hair. Yet again, he looked utterly golden, and to his aunt, he probably was. Dory snorted quietly. Cedric looked more serious. He was the older brother and carried the responsibility of the family and the title. The burden showed.

"I suppose Mr. Holmes is preparing the large table in the stateroom," Lady Pettifer said. "It is always so cold in there, even in summer. The fire is never enough."

"I believe so." The stateroom was used for more formal occasions and had a larger table that sat two dozen people if need be. It was a sumptuous room, showing the interest in everything Egyptian by some previous generation of the family.

"You better go down and help. I will be fine on my own," Lady Pettifer said. "Just return around five and help me dress."

"Of course," Dory said and bobbed a small curtsy. Dory hadn't informed her about what she'd learned about the scratches on a car. She'd been too busy to and it didn't seem the right time to talk about such things. Because it related to a family member, it was more difficult to discuss, but then there were some scratches. What relation could that have to Nora's death?

Dory went downstairs and with shortness, Mrs. Parsons sent her to Mr. Holmes to see if there was any assistance he needed. As per usual, Mr. Holmes was on the main family floor, seeing to Lord Wallisford and his guests. Dory entered the entrance hall through the discreet servant's entrance disguised in the paneling of the wall.

The guests were entering and Dory stood back. Animated men were laughing after their shooting session and a faint smell of gunpowder filled the hall as they walked in with their guns. Most walked through to the parlor, where a new round of drinks was in order. Dory stood back.

Vivian eventually walked in, smoking a cigarette. He said something to a man who chuckled, then he spotted her. Walking over, he stood before her. "Put this away, will you," he said, handing her the gun. The double barrels were still warm and the weapon was heavy. "Just doing our bit to charm Cedric's way," he said tartly, taking dark leather gloves off, finger by finger. Somehow, he didn't show any urgency to move away.

"Good shooting?" she asked, feeling she needed to address the silence.

He shrugged. "Not bad, if I say so myself. Growing up here, you learn to shoot. Particularly shooting pigeons off the roof. They make a hell of a mess. You also learn to manage the driest of company." Looking resigned, he walked into the parlor, and Dory watched him go. For seeming so comfortable in the company around him, he professed to loathe it. Maybe it was the lack of attractive women. Dory shook her head and took herself and her charge off to the gun cupboard, which had been left unlocked.

The parlor was abuzz with discussion and laughter when Dory made a discreet entrance and walked over to Mr. Holmes. She gently inquired if he needed her to do anything, noticing the mud that had been carried in across the carpet. As soon as the room was deserted again, that would have to be dealt with. "Just keep the drinks cabinet tidy," he requested of her.

Moving to stand by the drinks cabinet, she aligned glasses and decanters until it looked orderly. Ice still sat in the bucket and there wasn't much else for her to do just then, so she stood back and lowered her eyes.

Men were lounging across every sofa and chair with drinks in hand. Some of their boots still had mud on them and a couple of dogs milled around, walking from person to person. Vivian was chatting, looking animated and amused—completely different from the sentiments he'd expressed. His rebellious and outspoken nature wasn't on display for this group like it normally was. He pulled through for the family when needed.

"Chamberlain is assured to carry on Baldwin's policies," the man closest to her said, puffing on a cigar. As she noticed this, Mr. Holmes was already opening some of the windows. He anticipated everything. It was his job.

"There's no appeasing a tyrant. In the end, I don't think the policy is going to work. Hitler heeds no one—mark my words."

"Well, how much does a policy of appeasement count for when at the same time you're converting the largest factories in the country to churn out munitions. Hitler might not be the sharpest tool in the shed, but he's surely noticed."

"Churchill isn't helping, blathering on and on about Germany's building military strength."

"He is right, though. Any concession will only tell Hitler that our word means little, that we will fold on anything."

"Historically, his ambitions in Austria do have some justification."

"Not if you're Austrian."

"Quite a few would welcome him. Both Chamberlain and Baldwin are shutting their ears. It's pure scaremongering. It's criminal what Churchill is doing to the masses, terrifying everyone that Germans are going to march across Europe like locusts."

"I think what Chamberlain is doing is smart. He'll give appeasement a try, but keeps armament as a backup strategy. If war can be avoided, it is worth a few costs."

"A few countries, you mean?"

"Well, it's all talk, isn't it? Just because he has ambition doesn't mean it will happen. But there has to be a hard line at some point."

"As long as our alliance with the Russians holds, there will be control of his ambitions. The French to the west, the Russians to the east, there isn't too much room for him to maneuver, is there?"

"Well, the Italians are the big question. As long as they hold firm... But saying that, they are telling the League of Nations one thing and doing another. Can we really trust the damned Italians?"

The conversation carried on, talking about the Earl of Perth and difficulties in dealing with Mussolini. Dory hated hearing the threat of a war being discussed. It was too awful to contemplate. They were still recovering from the last one. Every family she knew carried the wounds of the last war. Just the idea of a new one was terrifying. These men made it sound as if they were facing an impossible position, and it was different from the things said on the radio, which were often quite complimentary about that

German and the policies he was instilling to strengthen his country's health and education.

Clearly there was a division amongst these men about how to deal with the Germans. Avoiding war was paramount and Dory wanted to believe with everything in her that Churchill was scaremongering. She hoped they were right and Hitler's ambition could be contained. But no one had failed to notice that refugees were appearing in scores in Dover, people that Hitler had deemed unwanted in his utopia.

The men in this room were a fair chunk of Britain's political guard. If anyone knew what they were talking about when it came to the state of the world, these men would. It was very distressing hearing what they had to say and the uncertainty with which they said it. Their lack of faith in Hitler to be reasonable didn't sound assuring. And if there was no certainty amongst these men, what hope had the rest of them?

Chapter 24

Because of the house guests, the staff didn't get their usual Sunday off. Technically, Dory could as Lady Pettifer wouldn't mind, but she didn't feel right leaving everyone else with a mountain of work while she wandered off for a day of leisure. So she put her day off until the guests were gone. Their stay had been endless work from dawn to midnight, and Dory felt exhausted.

When her day off finally came around, she slept until eleven, missing breakfast entirely. No doubt, Mrs. Parsons wouldn't approve, but that couldn't be helped, and a lie in was exactly what Dory needed.

The others were gone by the time she went downstairs and Dory stung at the disapproval that still came from the staff. They hadn't waited for her or approached her about what their plans were for the day. It could be that they hadn't meant to overtly overlook her, but it felt that way.

Larry had driven the girls in the car, so Dory wouldn't be going to Aylesbury unless she walked out to the road and waited for the bus. But Dory wasn't in the mood to go to Aylesbury. The travel would take most of the day and there was nothing she particularly needed. There was also the issue that she wanted to see DI Ridley. He hadn't come around while the guests had been here and Dory was curious about anything new he'd discovered.

Turning her attention to Nora's death also allowed her not to think about the incessant talk of war over the weekend.

With determination, she pedaled to Quainton, eager to be away from the Hall for a while and all the conflicting feelings she felt there. Of late, if felt as though she had been pummeled with emotions—fear of war, hurt at being fired and rejected, confusion over Vivian's hot and cold behavior, and generally dissatisfaction at being in domestic service in the first place. And she was homesick.

Having Gladys around helped, but Gladys was generally too busy to talk.

The town was quiet when she arrived. It being a weekday, people were off carrying on with their lives and business. For once, DI Ridley was in the constabulary office, sitting at the desk with a pencil between his teeth. His jacket was off and his sleeves rolled up. She stood there for a moment, watching him through the window, until he noticed being observed and she waved.

"Any developments?" she asked as she walked in. It wasn't a large office. Quainton only had one constable, and the office was essentially built for one.

"Nothing that is leading us any further," he said, leaning back and raking his fingers through his hair. "I'm running out of leads and running out of time."

That didn't sound encouraging. "Out of time?"

"With an investigation, I need to move ahead or start working on other things. The chief thinks it is time for me to go back to London."

"But we don't know who did it yet."

"And there is a possibility that we will never know."

That just sounded wrong. "We can't just give up."

"It's not giving up. It is simply allocating time until something new develops. It is the way of things, Miss Sparks. Care for some lunch at the pub? My treat."

Dory couldn't speak for a moment as conflicting thoughts were competing in her mind. Lunch. Did she want lunch? "Alright," she said and rose when he did. "When would you go back?"

"Well, if nothing new presents itself in the next day or so, then probably late Wednesday."

It was strange to think she wouldn't see him again. She had gotten used to seeing him around, to thinking about him and the investigation, and now it was over. He was getting ready to pack up and leave. "I'm sorry to hear that."

"So am I," he said, holding the door to the pub open for her. It was busy being lunch time, but not like it was on Sunday. A few people sat around the tables, some eating. "I think I'll have the bangers and mash today. You?"

Her mind was still not engaging properly and it took her a moment to think. "Venison pie."

He returned with a pint of ale and a lemon barley for her. It seemed he remembered what she liked to drink and it made her blush slightly, liking the idea that he remembered anything about her. "Well, I will not stop," she said and Ridley cocked his head to the side.

"You are not responsible for solving this murder. Sometimes things never get resolved. Sometimes the culprit doesn't get held to account. That is the nature of this, Dory."

It was the first time he'd used her first name and she liked how it sounded when he said it. "Nora Sands deserves to have her murderer found out."

"Don't make the mistake of carrying this as a personal burden. There is only heartache in that. I know this is difficult to hear, but we don't win every time."

Dory didn't want to hear it. "Still, I will keep trying while I am still around. Like you, I don't think I will be here all that long, at least not after Lady Pettifer leaves for

France. I will write to you with regards to any progress I make."

"Please do, but don't be zealous about this. There is a murderer around and if you present yourself as a zealous crusader, they might see you as a risk worth eliminating."

This was an uncomfortable thought and one Dory hadn't truly entertained before. It could well be that she had put questions to the actual murderer.

An elderly man in brown tweed sat down at the table next to them and took his cap off. Now it felt like Dory couldn't speak her mind anymore as there was someone close enough to listen in. He nodded to them and took a large swig of his ale. "DI Ridley," he said as greeting. "I hear you've been asking around the village about the Common Road."

"That's right," Ridley said.

"Some say it's haunted," the man continued.

"Haunted?" Ridley said with surprise.

"Had its victim, it has. Why are you asking about the Common Road?"

"Nora Sands was seen bicycling out there shortly before her demise and we cannot account for why. Do you live out that way?"

"Me? No, but the neighbor to my cousin had a gel that met a grisly end out on the Common Road. Not so long ago, either. Tilda was her name. Parents were devastated."

Ridley sat forward in his seat as if very interested. "When was this?"

"Not long ago, some months back. Fell into a ravine. Well, not really a ravine, a bank with a stream down below. They found her and her bicycle the next day after she didn't return. Died straight away."

A frown marred Ridley's brow. "I wasn't told about this."

"Well, you wouldn't have as it was an accident. Girl was always clumsy. Just got clumsy at the wrong time. Plus, technically, she was more a resident in Pitchcott than here. Still, very sad. The family is devastated, of course. Before that, there was a nasty accident between a tractor and a motorcycle, but that was some years back now. Grizzly, that was, too. That road has always been unlucky. They say the Royalists met the parliamentarians there back in the olden days. Soldiers still haunt the road."

"And what was Tilda's surname?"

"Turman it was. My sister married a Turman some twenty years ago. Only distant relation to Tilda, though."

The food arrived, but it was untouched for a moment. "Could these deaths be related?" Dory asked quietly after a while. The elderly man seemed to be lost in thought now, staring at the wall. The idea of falling down a ravine while bicycling was something Dory could relate to as she had been bicycling just a half an hour earlier. One day out for a bicycle ride and then dead. An image of Vivian zooming past her and almost knocking her off the road entered her mind.

"Scratches," she said in barely more than a whisper.

"I have found no connection between Nora Sands and Pitchcott." He turned his attention back to the man. "Do you know what happened to the bicycle?"

"I don't know. I suppose it returned to her parents, but it had gone down the ravine, so it won't be much good to anyone."

"Where exactly do they live?"

The man gave an address, then finished off his ale and placed the empty glass on the table. "I best get back," he said and rose, donning his cap again and tipping his fingers to it.

Ridley sat back again, his eyes off in the distance. "Care to come for a drive to Pitchcott?" he asked.

"Absolutely. This could be important."

"It could be. If Nora was interested in scratches on a car, then was seen out on the road where a girl was driven off, maybe she was investigating what happened to this girl. Mrs. Parsons said she was a curious girl, easily able to get herself into scrapes."

"Mrs. Parsons seems cursed with those girls," he said with a small smile as he returned his attention to his lunch. Dory knew full well there was a jibe at her in that statement.

Chapter 25

D I Ridley's car had the same blue color leather seat as the paint on the car itself. Dory waited by it while Ridley was inside making a phone call to the Pitchcott constable about this death a couple of months back. Eventually, he came outside and they got in. The car whined slightly as he drove, first through the village and then out onto the country lanes.

Dory didn't actually know where the Common Road was, but DI Ridley seemed to know where he was going.

"If Nora was investigating this death," Dory started, "it seemed she found the person responsible."

"If someone is responsible. There is nothing linking these two deaths as of yet. It may be that the death of Tilda Turman was accidental. Nora Sands might have had a completely different reason for being on the Common Road. Maybe she was going to Pitchcott, but we also have no evidence that she got there. The local constable is asking around to see if anyone had seen her."

"If she did meet one of the cars from Wallisford Hall, then that person wasn't driving from Aylesbury because they would have just come up through Waddesford, or up the Willows."

DI Ridley chewed his lip. "It is hard to say. It does suggest someone coming from or driving north, to

Bletchley perhaps, but it could also be someone driving south through Luton."

"But why would someone drive to London through Luton?" Dory asked.

"Until we have more details, we can't say."

They drove in silence for a moment, Dory trying to make this new information fit together inside her mind, but there were too many missing pieces. Being one of the family cars, it did suggest a family member, but it could have been someone else. Clearly, the car hadn't been stolen as it had been returned—scratched and damaged enough for George to deem it needed repairs. But there was no indication who had driven it.

They came across a parked car on the side of the road and a constable stood waiting with his rounded, black hat. Ridley pulled over and got out, and Dory followed suit.

"Constable Davis?" Ridley said and the man smiled. They shook hands and the constable nodded his greeting to her. "This is where it happened?"

"This is where she was found," the man said, walking over to the edge of the road. There was a small, stone wall, then a thirty-foot drop. "It took a couple of days searching to find her. Wasn't readily seen from the road down there." The low, stone wall was there to protect cars coming around the corner, but it hadn't protected Tilda. A chill rose up Dory's arms at the thought of the poor girl lying down there for days alone and unseen.

"She didn't suffer, did she?"

"No, broke her neck on the way down. Coroner said she was dead before she hit the ground."

Dory supposed that was some comfort.

"Why was she out here?" Ridley asked.

"Seeing to an elderly woman out at one of the farmhouses," the constable said. "Was on her way home, and never got there."

"That's awful," Dory commiserated, feeling the chill of the wind roaring across the landscape.

Crouching down, Ridley stroked his fingers along a scratch along the stone wall. As Dory looked closer, she could see flecks of blue along the scratch. "Is that paint?"

"Looks that way. I need some photos taken of this," Ridley said to the constable. "And a piece of the paint."

"I can organize that for you, sir," the constable said.

"And where is the bicycle?"

"Well, it was handed back to the family. If they kept it, I don't know."

It would be a gruesome keepsake if they did, Dory thought, again feeling sorry for this girl and her family. If Nora had been investigating this girl's death, then Dory felt a stronger respect for her. It certainly seemed like a plausible motive for her murder if she found that someone in the house was responsible. So, it wasn't one murder they were investigating, but two.

"We had better go ask them," Ridley said and nodded to the constable. Dory looked down the ravine again before following.

"Poor girl."

Ridley didn't say anything as he started the car and continued down the road.

"Do you think we have our motive?"

"I think that depends on if the bicycle was blue," he said, throwing her a glance. "If not, there was definitely a second vehicle involved."

"One of his lordship's cars is blue," Dory said. "It isn't the main one he uses. The Allard, I think it's called."

Ridley was chewing his lip again and they drove down the tight and winding road to Pitchcott. The village soon came into view. Well, it wasn't much of a village— just a church and some houses. As far as Dory could see, it didn't have a post office or even a pub. It was purely a farming village with not much else to it. There would be no reason Nora Sands would be coming here unless there was someone she was specifically visiting, but no one had ever mentioned that she knew anyone in Pitchcott.

The car swung in through a gate and they drove down a road through a field until they reached a farmhouse. This had to be where Tilda Turman lived with her family. A man stepped out into the yard with his thumb in his front pocket. He wore brown and green wool, and sturdy boots, curious to see what visitors had come to his farm and for what purpose.

"Mr. Turman?" Ridley said as he stepped out of the car.

"That be me," the man said.

Ridley introduced himself and quickly acknowledged Dory. The man nodded her way, but his eyes barely left DI Ridley's. "We were hoping we could have a look at Tilda's bicycle."

"Why'd you be wanting to look at Tilda's bicycle?" the man asked, a hint of suspicion in his eyes.

"To look at the damage. Do you still have it?"

"It's out the back," he said, indicating toward a building storing a tractor. The man walked away. He wasn't coming with them. Perhaps he didn't want to see it and be reminded of what had happened.

Ridley looked over at her and then started walking toward the edge of the building. Dory followed.

The grass was overgrown and there were all sorts of rusting equipment leaned up against the back of the building. On first sight, Dory saw no bicycle, but Ridley started moving to a lump covered with a brown tarp. Underneath was a bicycle, and clearly, it was brown in color.

"Not blue," Dory said.

"No, not blue," Ridley repeated absently.

The bicycle was an absurd shape, the front wheel bent and so was the handle bar. Detached spokes stuck out in impossible directions. As Dory watched, Ridley pulled out a magnifying glass and leaned closer. Then he stood up sharply and continued to take the tarp off it. "We need to take it with us," he said, lifting it up. Neither of the wheels rolled, the back section of the bicycle bent slightly. "Will you open the door of the car?"

"Of course," Dory said and ran ahead. She opened the back door and Ridley lifted it in.

"I'll just have a chat with Mr. Turman," he said and followed in the direction the man had gone. Dory took her seat in the front, turning slightly to look at the damaged bicycle. Whatever he'd seen with his magnifying glass had made him decide to take the bicycle with him.

It took an age for Ridley to come back, but he finally did.

"What did you see?" she asked when he stepped into the car and started the engine. "Did you see some blue paint?"

"It could have been. Hard to tell. We'll know more after it is properly examined."

Thoughts were racing through Dory's mind again. He wouldn't have taken it if he didn't suspect there was, or had seen what looked like blue paint. If confirmed, this meant a clear link between Tilda's bicycle and one of the Wallisford cars. Even just the paint on the stone wall suggested there was, but on the bicycle itself, it would be absolutely irrefutable.

This was the motive. This was the reason Nora had been murdered. She had seen the link between the scratches on the car and the death of this girl. Perhaps she had even found the paint on the stone wall like they had, had been out on this road to get that confirmation. Obviously, she had confronted someone with what she knew and been murdered for it. If only she hadn't been so secretive. She could be alive now, but she had kept it to herself and now she was dead.

"I'll take you home," Ridley said.

"But my bicycle."

"The constable will drop it off later. We've had enough bicycles on roads just lately," he said vaguely. In truth, she would be thinking of being run off the road the entire way back if she were to cycle. The previous incident of Vivian almost doing so returned to her mind. It had been so close, she had almost been knocked over by the sheer wind.

So this meant it could very well be Vivian responsible. He had a habit of driving fast and carelessly. The thought sat uncomfortably in her stomach.

Chapter 26

Ridley drove Dory straight to Wallisford Hall. They didn't speak much on the way back. To Dory's dismay, Ridley wasn't immediately going to question people at the Hall.

"It would be better if I knew for certain that there is paint on the wall and the paint on the bicycle, and if they are the same color as the car. Now, you go inside," he said. It wasn't so much a suggestion as an order and Dory couldn't do anything other than comply. He was a man used to giving orders by the ease in which he uttered them, expecting to be heeded.

As she watched, he walked toward the garage. Why couldn't she come with him?

Then he turned. "And Dory," he said. "It's best you let me handle things now. You've been instrumental, but we might be coming down to the nitty gritty now and things need to be done the proper way. Don't discuss what we've learned today with anyone. Promise me," he said.

Dory bit her lips together. In a way, she did understand that he wanted to get on with what he needed to do without interference, but it would be hard for her just to sit back and do nothing. This knowledge burned in her mind. "Fine, I won't discuss it with anyone," she said grudgingly, feeling as though she was being excluded from the most exciting part, left to go to her room like a chided child.

Ridley disappeared into the garage and Dory sighed. It had been an eventful day, a day that had had a significant development. They had established motive. Nora had been killed because she knew who had killed Tilda Turman. There was something very cruel and callous about that.

Dory entered an empty kitchen. Somehow, she'd expected Gladys to be there, but she wasn't. In her haste that morning, she hadn't actually asked Gladys what her plans were for the day. Lady Pettifer was out visiting again. In fact, the whole house seemed empty. Surely not everyone had left?

Grabbing a shortbread biscuit, Dory stood in the silent kitchen and ate. She really wanted a cup of tea, but couldn't be bothered boiling a pot just for herself. Perhaps she would wait for some of the others to return, but it would be hard to sit there and not tell people that she knew why Nora Sands had been murdered.

Someone in this house was responsible and goosebumps rose across her skin thinking about it. It had been someone who knew how to drive, so automatically that excluded Gladys, not that Gladys would ever murder someone. In fact, Gladys wouldn't be able to live with a guilty conscience for anything, let alone causing the death of some cyclist on the road.

One of the unanswered questions returned to Dory's mind. Where had this person come from? As far as she knew, most people here came and went from either

Aylesbury or London. Milton Keynes was up that way, but Dory didn't exactly know what else. Geography had never been her strong suit. Almost everything north of London was up there. What she really wanted was a map. It shouldn't prove impossible to find a map.

Dory stepped out of the kitchen and was met by nothing other than silence, so she walked up the stairs to the main family floor, and again, no one was around. Quietly, she walked across the main hallway and made her way to the library. She'd had to dust here every so often. Books created a surprising amount of dust.

The room was empty and quiet, dark cabinetry holding countless books. Some of them even looked medieval with worn and faded leather spines and gold writing. It took some time to find an Atlas, but she found a large, green book and brought it over to the table in the center of the room.

The initial map showed all of Britain, but didn't have enough detail. It took going through half the book before she found one that even showed Aylesbury. Quainton was a tiny dot, and Pitchcott wasn't even mentioned. With what she knew of the roads, she could identify the Willows, the A41, and the Common Road—in larger context, Pitchcott Road—she had learned that day, was to the north. A tiny line showed the road on the map. Moving her eyes, she saw Milton Keynes and Luton, but saw no reason why anyone would go there, unless it was one of the serving staff who had family there and thought nothing of stealing the family car for an outing to see their family. The idea seemed unlikely.

Moving her gaze along, her eyes settled on Cambridge. Milton Keynes sat between Quainton and Cambridge and there were certainly people in this family that had reason to go there.

With a slump, she sat down in a chair. It felt as though another thing had clicked into place. A creak alerted her that someone was around and she quickly closed the Atlas just as the door was opened.

"I thought I heard someone walking around," Vivian said in his bored and lazy tones. "What are you doing in here?"

"I was just looking for a book," she said, "on... birds."

"Birds?" Vivian said with surprise.

"I saw a strange one. Red chest and yellow beak." Her voice sounded thin, even to her own ears. She had never been an accomplished liar.

"You're asking the wrong person. Unless I can shoot it, I pay little attention to birds. Never took you for a budding ornithologist."

Dory didn't exactly know what the word meant, but got the gist of it. In fact, she knew nothing about birds, shooting worthy or not, but it was the excuse that popped into her head.

"You should go before Mother sees you in here. She's not really the liberal kind if you hadn't noticed."

Dory had noticed, alright. Lady Wallisford liked clear distinction between family and servant. Vivian seemed less fussed, or perhaps that only applied to certain maids. Dory refused the blush that threatened to color her cheeks.

She would not blush for a man like Vivian. "I understand there is a department that studies such things at Cambridge. They have taxidermized animals of all sorts, I have heard."

"Not really my area, but I'm sure they do. Natural science or something of that ilk. Why do you ask?" There was a curious suspicion in his eyes, as though this conversation was completely unexpected. She probably was making a complete hash job of this.

"No reason," she said, standing up. "You must get homesick when you are there."

He snorted. "Truthfully, I spend as little time here as I have to. I'm certainly not going to run home in the middle of term for the comforts of home fires burning." Sarcasm laced his voice.

"So you didn't come home this last term at all?"

"I only come home when they kick me out at the end of the year. And Christmas, of course. Not even I can avoid Christmas, although I have tried on occasion. Mother won't have it and she can be a pain in the arse when she wants something."

"Oh," Dory said with a frown. Was it true that he had not come home at all since Christmas?

"What are you up to, Miss Sparks?"

"Nothing," Dory said. "Just making conversation."

He didn't look appeased.

"As you say, I should make myself scarce before your mother sees me."

"Good idea," he said, his eyes following her as she quickly placed the Atlas back. "Although you won't find many birds in there."

"I gave up. Turned my attention to what I will do for my holidays."

"And what have you decided?"

"I haven't yet."

"Some seaside holiday park?" he said with derision.

"You know us working-class people. We love our seaside holidays," she said tartly. Never had she been on one, but the derision in his voice made her hackles rise and she couldn't help being a little acerbic back.

Dory left the room without another word. If it were true that Vivian hadn't left Cambridge during the term, he could not be responsible—unless he knocked a girl off the road and then decided to not carry on with his intended journey. But the car had been taken and returned to the garage, so it categorically couldn't be him. It had to be someone else. It could even be George, who had full and unencumbered access to the cars. He could have lied about not knowing where the scratches came from.

Vivian, the most likely suspect in her mind was ruled out. She really should let Ridley know about this. He would likely tell her off for doing exactly what he'd asked her not to do, but she had been quite clever about it, not revealing a thing of what they'd learnt. Still, he wouldn't be happy, but this information was more important than DI Ridley's displeasure. Once he spotted the connection with Cambridge, he would assume Vivian was responsible, too.

Dory just had to establish if what Vivian said was true, and that shouldn't be difficult. Even Gladys would know if Vivian had returned from university at any point during the term. Somehow Dory expected that he had told her the truth.

Chapter 27

"How are you, dear?" Lady Pettifer asked when Dory arrived in her room. "I hope you had an interesting day."

"I did," Dory said, busying herself by folding some of Lady Pettifer's clothes. "How was Lady Hallstaff?"

"Suffers from her ailments. Ever since she was a young woman, she has suffered from ailments. They're all in her head, of course. She's healthy as a horse, but refuses to acknowledge it."

Dory nodded absently.

"Did you see that handsome detective in the village, by any chance?" she asked, her eyes piercing Dory from where she sat by the window with a book in her lap. Against her own will, Dory blushed. "Still milling around, it seems."

"Yes," Dory said, clearing her throat.

"He must still believe there are some means of solving this murder," Lady Pettifer continued. Dory still felt the woman's attention on her and Dory turned away. The truth was that the investigation was increasingly pointing in the direction of the family, and that was something Lady Pettifer would not like hearing. "Did he mention any developments to his investigation?"

Dory continued to burn red, keeping her face away from Lady Pettifer.

"Come on now, Dory, spit it out. I can tell you know something."

With a sigh, Dory turned around. What was the point in lying? DI Ridley wasn't going to hide the fact that DI Ridley's attention had turned to the lordship's Allard. Sitting down heavily, she looked at Lady Pettifer, not wanting to be the one to bring this news to her. "It seems, or DI Ridley suspects, that one of Lord Wallisford's cars was involved in an incident on the road a few months back where a girl was killed."

The frown on Lady Pettifer's face was so deep that her eyebrows looked as one. "And what's led him to believe this?"

"Well, this road was where Nora Sands was seen cycling."

"The Common Road," Lady Pettifer cut in.

"It is believed that Nora was looking into this, hence the interest she had shown in Michael Jones' work repairing cars."

Lady Pettifer rose from her position and paced, her fingers pressed to her mouth.

"There appears to be paint on a stone wall near the site where the girl was run off the road and on the bicycle the girl was on at the time, that could potentially to have come from the lordship's Allard. And I am also breaking his confidence by telling you this." It didn't feel good, but her loyalty felt divided between Ridley and Lady Pettifer. She and Lady Pettifer had been partners in their interest in what had happened to Nora Sands.

With this news, Lady Pettifer gasped. "It can't be true," she stated. "Any blue car could be responsible for what happened to that girl." The weakness in her voice showed that she wasn't anywhere near certain about what she was saying.

"I am sure DI Ridley is making inquiries about all blue cars that have been repaired in the district recently."

"It doesn't have to be in the district. Anyone could be traveling through."

"Yes, but who would be driving down Pitchcott Road if they weren't going to Quainton?"

The deep frown remained on Lady Pettifer's brow and Dory felt awful having to bring this news. DI Ridley was homing in on the family and there was no question about it. Again, it could be that someone else had driven the car, but really, would any of the servants simply borrow a car? Larry and some of the gardeners drove, but they would never dream of taking the Allard.

"Leave me," Lady Pettifer urged. "I don't think I will be going down to supper tonight. I feel a headache coming on."

Still feeling awful, Dory did as she was asked, silently closing the door as she left Lady Pettifer's room.

"What's wrong with you?" Mavis asked as Dory walked further down the hall. "You look like you've seen a ghost."

Dory tried to smile. "It's just been a long day. Are you ready to go downstairs and help with supper?"

"Is Lady Pettifer not coming down?"

"No, she is going to stay in her room."

"We better tell Gladys to prepare a tray for her."

Dory nodded and followed Mavis down the servants' staircase to the basement. It felt like the house had a heavy atmosphere. People knew that DI Ridley had been spending time in the garage, and even if they couldn't guess the reason, they knew he had found something—something that was leading back to the house.

*

With Clara taken down by a cold, Dory offered her service to help with the family supper. After the visit with the party of politicians and other notables, her service wasn't quite as offensive as it used to be. It was an improvement in relations between her and the rest of the staff. Still, it wasn't entirely comfortable and Dory spent much more time in her room than she used to.

The family was quiet during supper that night. It was as if none of them wanted to speak to each other. Livinia was the only one trying to make conversation, but no one responded with more than a word or two, and eventually she gave up too with a great sigh.

Vivian was downcast, barely looking up from the table where he studiously eyed his wine glass. He wasn't holding back with the wine and Mr. Holmes had to refill his glass repeatedly.

As he often did, he completely ignored Dory when she brought his plate over from the serving table.

"I hear the Mawstaffs are in residence at the moment," Lady Wallisford stated, breaking the heavy silence.

"Oh," Lord Wallisford responded, as if pleased there was something to discuss. The scowl on Livinia's face only deepened when it became apparent that her topics were of no interest, but the pointless movements of the Mawstaffs were. "He's coming back for the hunting season. Never was much of hunter. Aim's shot. Can't hit a thing further than thirty yards, and he's struggling even at that."

Dory listened while she worked. Someone around this table had murdered Nora Sands—Dory was sure of it. And chances were that they were driving to Cambridge.

If Vivian's assertion that he hadn't left all term was true, then it wasn't him. Livinia hadn't been around while Tilda was murdered, which left three—Lord Wallisford, Lady Wallisford and Cedric.

Cedric ignored her as she placed his plate down, which wasn't surprising as he never paid any heed to the staff. Did any of them actually care that Nora was dead and that one of them had stuck a knife in her back?

Mr. Holmes was watching her like a hawk, as if suspecting that she was plotting something. There was a murderer in the house and she was the one treated with suspicion because she wanted to find out who was responsible.

For a moment, she wondered if she should just leave, but it felt as though she was letting the murderer win. Ridley was homing in on the culprit and Dory felt sure it was only a matter of time now. It shouldn't prove impossible to discover who had driven the Allard.

Chapter 28

Ridley didn't appear again for a few days and Dory was starting to wonder what had happened. Surely he wasn't ending the investigation now that they were homing in on the culprit, but eventually, he did appear again, driving up to park right at the front entrance. That would likely bother a few people in the house, being the spot for honored guests when he was anything but.

Mr. Holmes was left to deal with him and Dory gave him a quick wave from the landing above. He didn't give her more than a cursory glance and a tiny nod before being led into the parlor.

"Must we be harassed by this infernal man forever?" Lady Wallisford asked as she walked past with Livinia. Dory turned her head away from them and busied herself with the wilting bouquet on a table.

"He wishes to speak to us, Mama," Livinia said with her typical bored tone.

"Yes, but there should be a limit to how much of our time he can command." They continued down the stairs and into the parlor; Dory only hearing mumbled voices prior to the door closing.

They stayed for about ten minutes and then it was Vivian's turn. Dory returned to Lady Pettifer, finding her sitting at her table, writing a letter. "I understand Detective Ridley is here again."

"Yes, he's in the parlor, currently questioning Vivian."

Lady Pettifer sighed. There had been a distinct cooling in the relationships between Dory and Lady Pettifer since Dory had revealed the findings around the car. Dory was sorry for it, but there was nothing she could do to change it. It wasn't, after all, her fault, even though she sometimes felt as though people were assigning blame to her. The old adage of the messenger being at risk of being shot really was true, but what was she supposed to do— ignore everything and hope the culprit was never caught? If that was a requirement for working here, she was better off elsewhere.

"Poor Vivian," Lady Pettifer said. "He's barely more than a boy."

"He says he never left Cambridge all term, which Ridley should be able to establish."

The answer didn't seem to comfort Lady Pettifer. "This constant suspicion and accusation will ruin the family."

Dory tried to keep her expression cool. She had expected more from Lady Pettifer—that she would care about justice for Nora above how the family was perceived, but apparently not. Perhaps Dory was expecting too much.

"It is all just awful," Lady Pettifer continued. She was quiet for a moment. "And Cedric?"

Turning slightly, Dory shrugged. "I don't know. DI Ridley will establish his whereabouts, I suppose."

Lady Pettifer worried her lip. "He's so young. Had his whole life in front of him. This all is giving me the most tremendous nerves." The lady had been very interested in this investigation——until it started pointing to a member of her family. Dory supposed she could understand. Someone was going to be caught for this and they would hang. It was hard to consider that happening to a family member, seeing such an outcome advance like an unstoppable train wreck.

"I'm sorry," Dory said after a while.

"It's not your fault," Lady Pettifer said with a labored smile. "There are no winners in a situation like this and the suffering is spread far and wide. It is an inordinately selfish act, murdering someone. Now go see what is happening downstairs."

In a way, Dory didn't want to. She felt like she'd had enough of this investigation. It wasn't fun and exciting anymore. As they were coming closer to the truth, something very ugly was emerging, even if it wasn't entirely clear yet. But she nodded and left the room, returning to the landing about the main entrance, where she polished the rich, red wood of a mahogany table. If Mr. Holmes or Mrs. Parsons challenged her for being there, she would have to think of something to say. She was here on Lady Pettifer's orders after all, but it wouldn't do anything good for her standing downstairs.

Cedric emerged from the parlor and it was Lord Wallisford's turn, who Dory could tell, even from up high, that he was thoroughly offended. He had a way of holding himself tall when he felt his due respect wasn't shown. DI Ridley's mandate couldn't take into account such position.

A bang almost made Dory knock over the polish.

"This is utterly stupid," a sharp voice said. Dory knew it was Vivian. He emerged from the salon on the other side. "I'm sick of being tugged around like a puppet in a show. Being subjected to one moron after another. When is this charade going to end?" He marched up the stairs. "And you," he said when reaching the landing. "Always skulking around, looking for something titillating to entertain you. I hope you're getting a real show. How have they not managed to fire you yet?"

His accusing voice boomed and echoed off the walls of the cavernous space. Mr. Holmes' sharp and piercing eyes bored into her from downstairs. Dory opened her mouth as if unable to say anything. What could she say—that she was only here because Lady Pettifer asked her to be?

He wasn't finished. "You really think too much of yourself. You're just a stupid maid and a damned useless one at that." He threw her a disgusted look as if she was something nasty and smelly that had crawled out of the sea.

Throughout his tirade, he hadn't even slowed down, simply kept marching down a corridor until he turned the corner. Dory didn't know what to do. She had never been addressed like that before—her intelligence, purpose and usefulness entirely dismissed in one go. Perhaps not entirely true as it had happened roughly the same when she had spilled tea on the executive from London in her last job. She had spent days dissecting every word of the tirade, burning with shame and offense. At the time, she'd felt it had been an unnecessary cruelty.

Seeking titillating entertainment was what he accused her of. The unjustness of it burned inside her chest. Firstly, he was giving himself too much credit for thinking she cared about his monstrous and stupid family. They were all awful—especially him, who had at some points even seemed to be friendly. Well, he had the potential to be friendly, although perhaps that was him trying to charm her into lowering her guard. If she actually had, she would be devastated now by a tirade like that. She had been utterly right not to trust him. When the pressure was on, he treated her like dirt under his shoe.

The accusation still sat in Mr. Holme's eyes. She could feel him watching her. He would never address her in view of the family, or on the family floor, but there would be some point later downstairs when he would dress her down, reminding her what the proper code of conduct was—probably remind her again that if he had the means to fire her, he would. It didn't matter if Vivian Fellingworth was being mean and spiteful, accusing her of vile things that weren't true. The family was always right in their view.

Vivian appeared again, still marching. This time he stared past her as if she wasn't there, carrying a leather bag with him as he made his way down the stairs and toward the front door, which he slammed loudly as he left. His car wailed to life and sped off in a roar.

No doubt she would be accused of driving him from the house as well.

"Was that Vivian?" Livinia asked, emerging from the salon. "What's put a bee in his bonnet? Always one for dramatics, isn't he?"

Mr. Holmes didn't reply, but Dory was fairly certain he blamed her as if she was personally responsible for Vivian's mood swings and bad behavior. Anything to not blame the family and the people responsible for their own behavior. For some reason, it seemed appropriate to blame her.

Lord Wallisford appeared. "I need to make a phone call in my study, Holmes. Ensure I'm not disturbed." With a gruff grunt, he disappeared, and Dory felt it was a good time to do so herself, before Mr. Holmes decided it was time to have a little talk.

Grabbing her bottle of polish and cloth, she decided to move along to a table out of view of the main entrance. The insults and accusations thrown her way still burned. And it wasn't just from Vivian—he was just the latest. Lady Wallisford had accused her. So had Mr. Holmes and Mrs. Parsons. It was as though if she went away, all the problems here would too—as if she personified the rot in this house. Didn't that just make her the ultimate scapegoat? Luckily, she hadn't been here at the time or they would all be trying to pin this murder on her.

Chapter 29

"**M**y presence downstairs wasn't appreciated," Dory confessed when she returned to Lady Pettifer's room. "I am being accused of interfering."

"By who?"

"Everyone."

"What happened? You look close to tears."

She was close to tears. A painful lump burned in her throat. "Maybe it's time for me to leave."

"Nonsense. You can't let people chase you away. Sit down, Dory," she ordered and Dory did as she was told, sitting down on the edge of the bed. She felt like a child about to be admonished—yet again. "You can't take it to heart that things are unpleasant. Something awful has happened and it takes something awful in return to sort it out."

"It is as though everyone feels this should be swept under the carpet and are angry with me for not being complicit."

"Not allowing something to be swept under the carpet is what makes you a stronger person, Dory. None of this is pleasant, but justice needs to be done. The person responsible should be the one bearing the brunt of it. Not you."

"Even if it's someone from the family?" Dory challenged, even though she didn't want to.

Lady Pettifer sighed. "I have been unfair to you, haven't I?"

"Out of quite a few people here, you have been the kindest."

"This is going to end unpleasantly and for the rest of us, that takes some preparation. I'm sorry if I was short with you. In no way are you responsible for this person's actions or the consequences coming back to roost."

"Some have accused me of finding entertainment in all this."

Lady Pettifer raised her eyebrow. "Vivian, I take it."

Dory didn't want to confirm, but she wasn't about to lie and deny it either.

"He does have a tendency to lash out, but we must be understanding of Vivian and the position he's in."

Dory just about snorted when Lady Pettifer continued, the woman's gaze lost out the window. "I think he knows who's responsible, and I think he's known for some time. Growing up, he used to be so proud of his family and their position. He never questioned the rightness of any of it, but lately, particularly with this, all those perceptions have been challenged. It is a harsh thing to realize the people you respected and believed in are not what you thought they were."

Although how anyone could live in this house and not see how awful these people were was beyond Dory, but she guessed she understood what Lady Pettifer was saying.

"My brother always stands for pomp and ceremony, but at times focuses more on the spectacle than the underlying substance. Things are about to unravel, and we all know it. Just how it does so, we are yet to see."

*

Being seen with DI Ridley only added fuel to the fire, but Dory was beyond caring. There was nothing salvageable with her relationship with the family and the other staff. Mavis was still guardedly civil, but Clara was giving Dory the cold shoulder, ignoring her presence like most of the others. Clearly, she had put a foot wrong—or several, and was being censured. It was a censure she refused to accept.

Gladys was caught in the middle and it obviously caused her some distress, and Dory was sorry for it, but there were bigger concerns here than the politics in the house. Crime and punishment had and was unfolding before their very eyes. Putting their heads in the sand and ignoring it wasn't going to achieve anything.

Walking outside through the basement door, Dory found DI Ridley walking along the gravel and smoking a cigarette. He looked worried, or she assumed it was worry. It was still inordinately difficult to read him.

As he noticed her, he smiled briefly and Dory returned the gesture. "How goes the questioning?"

A lopsided smile tugged the corner of his mouth and he dropped the cigarette, grinding it into the gravel with his foot. "They are circling the wagons, as they say. They're all stonewalling me. I think they got together and all decided on a strategy. I'm getting nothing out of them. No one can remember anything."

"Maybe you'll have better luck with the staff, although I doubt any of them would be happy to talk to you."

"Are they giving you a hard time for helping me?"

Dory's lack of an answer was answer enough. "I think my time here is done."

"We are so close," Ridley said, distracted by his thoughts. "There are just one or two pieces left and it all comes together. The question is who was driving the car. George Henry does not know, but all family members know how to drive."

"And some staff. We know it's not Vivian, Livinia, Cedric or Lady Pettifer. The only people who were around during both incidents were Lady and Lord Wallisford," Dory said. "Vivian was away all term and never returned—"

"But he was here when Nora Sands was killed."

Dory watched him intently, trying to understand what he was saying and what it meant. "You mean the same person wasn't responsible for Nora and Tilda."

"We cannot say that with certainty."

That changed things. "Then we know that Cedric, Livinia and Lady Pettifer were not here when Nora was murdered. Lady Pettifer wasn't here before, either."

"She is the only person who can have no involvement."

"So, we really are no further along than we were."

Ridley was silent, his fingers stroking along his brow. "I have made some inquiries at Cambridge and we'll see what returns. If someone drove there and back, there might be some record of it. Then we will know who was driving. Unfortunately, no one in Quainton has any memory of seeing anyone from the village drive past around that time, or don't remember now."

There was still a chance this would be unsolved. "Lady Pettifer seems to think Vivian knows who's responsible."

"I don't doubt it. Look, Dory, I think you need to stay out of sight as much as possible. There is a murderer in this house and they must be feeling pressure now—the kind of pressure that makes people irrational and dangerous. You are the one in the house and many here see you as complicit in this investigation. Now is not the time to put yourself in front of everyone for attention. Ideally, you should leave."

"I'm not leaving Lady Pettifer in the lurch." That was only partially true. Dory wanted to see this through to the end. It would prey on her mind for the rest of her life if she left now, even if she eventually found out how things resolved. She didn't want to be sent away like a naughty child. It would also feel like handing victory to the people who were all too willing to sweep Nora's death under the carpet for whatever misplaced sense of propriety and service. Truthfully, Dory couldn't understand it, but she did get Ridley's point. Who knew what level this person would go to in their desperation to conceal themselves?

"I will stay clear and only deal with Lady Pettifer," she promised. With their interaction that morning, Dory felt as though they had cleared some of the tension between them. Dory did understand the pressure and discomfort this was causing. This person's actions had and would bring suffering to everyone. Even the staff would suffer in the long run. Who would want a servant who came from such a notorious position? The same was true for her. A letter of recommendation from the house of Lady or Lord Wallisford wouldn't serve her terribly well either, Dory thought with a chuckle. Good thing domestic service was not for her.

"If anything strange occurs, anything out of the norm, I want you to run. Get out and take to the forest if need be. Just be out of reach."

Surely, it wasn't as serious as all that, but then he was the policeman. He knew much more about what could happen than she did.

"It would bother me immensely if you got hurt as a result of all this," he said, again in that absent way in which he sometimes spoke, as if thinking aloud.

The statement surprised Dory and she felt uncomfortable at the consideration. No one had ever shown such concern for her before and it was all the more confrontational because it was him. It wasn't as if he'd particularly shown any great concern, but apparently, it was more than she had assumed. "Anything untowards and I will run like the devil."

He smiled, watching her for a moment and Dory felt the pit of her stomach drop. She absolutely should not be taking a fancy to this man, who would only be in her life for another few days. Either this case would be solved or he would be recalled to London.

Maybe that wasn't the end of the world. Who was to say she couldn't go to London after this, find a new opportunity and a new career? It made sense to turn her attention to London. They might very well see each other again. A deepening blush crept up her cheeks.

Chapter 30

DI Ridley returned the next day, questioning some of the staff, but his activities were disturbed by the arrival of several cars, one of them including the Commissioner of Police. Dory watched it with Lady Pettifer from the window. She had no idea who the man was, but Lady Pettifer did.

"Do you think DI Ridley has involved the Commissioner of Police?" Dory asked. "Is this typical?" It seemed extraordinary.

"I'd say not," Lady Pettifer said. "I suspect this is my brother's doing." She wore a grave expression on her face as she let the lace curtains drop back into place.

"Your brother has called the Commissioner of Police," Dory said disbelievingly. "Ridley said they were stonewalling him. Why would they purposefully call in the top policeman of all?"

"Because the situation has become untenable, I would guess. This is damage control." Lady Pettifer sat down heavily at the dressing table. "Perhaps he is hoping the Commissioner will make things go away. They know each other. Go see what is happening," Lady Pettifer said.

Dory swallowed the discomfort constricting her throat at the assignment. Last time she had been told to go spy, things had gone disastrously—cementing the chasm between her and the rest of the staff. Well, what was the point of worrying now? There was the warning DI Ridley had given her to stay out of sight, but curiosity got the better of her. The Commissioner of Police had turned up out of the blue. This had to signify something monumental. "Fine," she said guardedly.

With effort, she could be discreet about this, and hopefully, no other people would cast accusation at her feet, or in her face, as was Vivian Fellingworth's style. Gingerly, she walked down the hall toward the landing above the main entrance.

"You shouldn't go there," Mavis said, her voice a harsh whisper. Dory hadn't seen her.

"Lady Pettifer wants to know what's going on."

Mavis sighed, her eyes as large as saucers. Even she sensed something serious was occurring. "Are they policemen?" she asked as they approached the landing and peeking around the corner. The entrance hall was filled with men. Some uniformed, but the man who looked like the Commissioner wasn't. He greeted Lord Wallisford as if seeing an old friend. What they were saying couldn't be heard, but they spoke with serious expressions before retreating into the study. The men stayed in the hall, seemingly with nothing to do but to look around.

"It is the Commissioner of Police," Dory said, "and his men, I suppose."

"The Commissioner?" Mavis said with surprise, exactly like Dory had done not so long ago. It was an outlandish concept on first hearing. "Is he here to help with the investigation?"

The answer was that Dory didn't think so. There was a knot in her stomach that grew tighter. But then maybe the Commissioner got involved when crime included prominent members of the aristocracy. Perhaps this wasn't surprising at all. Then again, Lady Pettifer's reaction suggested something less straightforward.

Ridley appeared, having been summoned and he was called to the study. It was quiet downstairs, everyone there was excluded from the conversation going on behind closed doors. Mr. Holmes was standing completely expressionless, but Dory could tell he didn't like all these intruders in the house.

She drew her head back before she was noticed. There was no point observing until something was happening. Mavis was standing with her hands to her mouth. "They know who the murderer is, don't they?" She looked shaken as if the thought of there being a murderer in the house had just occurred to her.

"I don't know," Dory said honestly.

The door opened and Dory peeked past the corner again. Ridley was leaving through the main doors. He wasn't going back downstairs to finish his interviews; he was leaving. In her heart, she knew he wasn't coming back.

Dory ran to the servants' staircase and flew downstairs, through the basement and out the kitchen door.

Rounding the corner of the house, she saw him walking toward his car, the length of his coat flaring in the wind. When he turned toward the car door, she could see the drawn and unhappy expression on his face. Whatever had occurred in the study, he wasn't happy about it.

"You're leaving?" Dory asked.

"I've been taken off the case."

"How can they do that? This is your case."

"It is the Commissioner's case now. I have been told to relinquish everything to do with this case and return to London immediately."

"They can't do that."

"It is the Commissioner. What he says goes."

Dory didn't know what to say, or what this meant. "They're just going to sweep it away?"

"I don't know," Ridley said. "He didn't tell me what he intends to do." There was a bitterness in his voice.

"This can't be right. We must tell the papers or something. They can't just get away with it."

"It's not my concern anymore," Ridley said tightly. "You should leave here," he said before stepping into his car and closing the door. The car started, but he didn't drive off yet; instead, he rolled down the driver's window. "It was Cedric that drove the car that pushed Tilda Turman off the road. The administration at Cambridge confirmed he'd been invited and attended a luncheon there. He had been drinking a fair bit from what I was told."

Rolling up the window again, he gave her a salute before driving off down the long road through the estate. Cedric, Dory repeated in her head. Cedric was responsible, but he had definitely not been here when Nora died, so Ridley had been right; the two incidents were not committed by the same person.

Crossing her arms around her, Dory didn't know what to do. Everything had turned upside down, and now they knew partially who was responsible, the family had called for reinforcements in guise of the Commissioner. Surely they couldn't simply ignore this?

Guardedly, Dory returned to the house and went straight to Lady Pettifer's room, partially because she wanted to be out of sight, but also because she felt she had to impart what she'd just learnt with Lady Pettifer.

Dory found her sitting by the window, looking calm and collected.

"Detective Ridley has been dismissed," Dory said as the woman looked at her expectantly. "Lord Wallisford and the Commissioner are conferencing in the study." Well, they had been last she had seen.

"I see," Lady Pettifer said, putting her hands together.

Taking a breath, Dory steadied himself. "And he said," and she wasn't entirely sure he was allowed to impart this knowledge, "that it was Cedric that had been driving the car that forced Tilda Turman off the road, that he had been to a luncheon at Cambridge and he'd been drinking."

Lady Pettifer remained still and silent, her mouth drawn tight. She blinked a couple of times. "I see," she said again. "But he wasn't responsible for Nora."

"No. Can they really hide this?" Dory asked. "Can the Commissioner just make the whole investigation go away?"

"The Commissioner is an honorable man," Lady Pettifer said. "My brother has obviously decided that he needs to take this in hand. He can be willfully ignorant when he can get away with it, but he's not a stupid man.

206

Oh, Cedric, you stupid, stupid boy. If he'd just done the right thing and reported his accident and the consequences to that poor girl, none of this would have happened."

Livinia burst through the door, making Dory's heart stop with the suddenness of it. Tears were flowing down her cheeks. "What is happening? They're saying they're here because Mama is responsible for this heinous thing."

To Dory, this couldn't be more shocking, but Lady Pettifer wasn't surprised. She'd already identified who the culprit was. Lady Wallisford had murdered Nora Sands. The truth was too astounding to process.

Livinia was overwrought. "I don't understand. Do something. Papa needs to do something," the girl said as she flew into her aunt's lap. The confident and arrogant girl Dory had always seen was gone now—now crying uncontrollably. Lady Pettifer stroked her head.

"They're saying she killed that girl. I don't believe it. How could they say such vile things?" Livinia sobbed and Lady Pettifer sighed.

Dory felt out of place, as if she shouldn't be witnessing this. Things weren't exactly being swept under the carpet, it seemed. Lady Wallisford was being accused, and what evidence they have, Dory didn't know. The woman had killed Nora because Nora had found out about Cedric's accident, and Nora must have confronted Lady Wallisford with it.

Cedric's accident hadn't been intended, even if he was fully culpable, so it wasn't as if he would hang for it, but Lady Wallisford had felt it was worth murdering the accuser rather than let it come to light. The callousness of it stung. Poor Nora, having lost her life in seeking justice for Tilda Turman.

Chapter 31

The Commissioner and his men left without carting anyone off. Lady Wallisford had taken to her room and refused to come out, being tended to by Mavis for all meals. Livinia stayed in her room, and Cedric sat and smoked in the library. Otherwise, the house was quiet. No one seemed to know what was going on or what they should do, so the staff went about their business as if nothing had happened.

There was a general silence in the house where no one spoke and no one seemed to want the company of anyone else. The house felt drained of all energy, as if a battle had been commenced and lost. Dory felt drained as well. She tended to Lady Pettifer and stayed in her room where they seldom spoke. No one came or went from the house. Vivian stayed away wherever it was he had gone.

In the afternoon, Lady Pettifer conferred with the lordship inside his study for a good hour and Dory could tell that something had been decided. Soon after, Cedric was called in and the discussion continued. Dory didn't get to see him come out again because she needed to see to Lady Pettifer.

"Lady Wallisford is to be sent to Switzerland," she said when they entered her room. "A sanitorium."

Dory absorbed the news.

"She's not mad, of course—just ambitious and ruthless. One should perhaps understand that she was protecting the reputation and future of her son—but to murder an innocent girl... That really is beyond the pale. My brother has agreed with the Commissioner that she be sent away." She wasn't looking at Dory, instead twisting the bottles of perfume and face cream on her dresser. "Maybe one has to be a bit mad to do what she did. It may be less than she deserves, but it would be difficult to hang a lady. This is seen as a better solution. She will be trialed in absentia. It will be quick and there will be a scandal. Cedric will have to account for his part in this. There will be some reparations to the family, I expect."

Standing where she was, Dory didn't know how to respond. In a way, Lady Wallisford was getting off with a much lighter sentence than anyone else would, but she was to lose her family, her standing and her freedom. No doubt the environment will be nicer than anything she would experience at His Majesty's pleasure, but it was still punishment. What impact this would have on Cedric's political career, Dory didn't dare guess.

"And you, my dear," Lady Pettifer said, looking at her through the mirror.

"Me?"

"Your part in this investigation has hardly gone unnoticed."

"I didn't really do anything," Dory said, "beside speak to a handsome detective every once in a while."

Lady Pettifer smiled, but the events were too recent for there to be much levity to it. "We have discussed what to do with you."

Dory frowned. What to do with her? What was there to do with her? "I assumed I would be leaving. I don't think there can be any question of staying."

Lady Pettifer shifted her head as she considered Dory. "The scandal will, of course, mean that you will be hounded by journalists. This will be quite a scandal, made much worse if someone discusses it. Everyone will want to hear your account of this."

Swallowing, Dory looked away. She hadn't anticipated this, but now that Lady Pettifer mentioned it, it was logical. Dory had no interest in speaking about this to journalists, her name and picture in the papers. People whispering as she passed on the street. That sounded awful. "I have no interest in speaking of this."

"I didn't think so, but your life could become quite unpleasant here for a while—at least until things blow over. Hence, I think it is best that you come with me for a while—to France."

Dory blinked. "France?"

"I don't need a maid, but you can be my companion. It is a frightfully old-fashioned position, but I think you would enjoy it. It shouldn't prove onerous for you."

Images flashed through her mind, but she really had no idea what to expect.

Lady Pettifer continued. "I hadn't intended on leaving for another month, but circumstances suggest we should be flexible. My brother is to take Cedric up to Scotland for the shooting season. Livinia will come with us. Wallisford Hall will be closed down probably until next year. It is up to you, of course, if you wish to come or not. It would be a pleasure to have you, and it will give you a chance to work on your French."

"My French is poor."

Lady Pettifer smiled. "You'll have a long sea journey to brush up on it. Think about it and give me your answer tomorrow. We will be leaving very soon." With a dismissive nod, Dory was asked to leave and she did.

France. What an outlandish notion. What in the world would she do in France, and what did a companion do? Still, it was an opportunity to see the world outside of Swanley and Quainton. The thought of journalists hounding her everywhere she went, made the idea of going to London much less attractive. The idea of them milling around outside her mother's house was even worse. Perhaps in her wisdom, Lady Pettifer had arranged a merciful alternative.

Dory was going to France. Excitement bubbled up like nervousness in her belly. It was nice to see something beyond the heaviness that plagued this house and the despicable act that had ended a young woman's life for reasons Dory could never truly get her head around. It seemed so outrageous. But then she didn't want to spend more time thinking of Lady Wallisford and her dark, selfish motives. Too much of her time had been dedicated to it and now it was a pleasure to think of something else. France. Who would have thought?

*

Lady Wallisford was taken away the next day. George had been asked to prepare the car and it stood waiting outside for her to emerge from the house. This was a family event, so no staff were in attendance other than George. Even Mr. Holmes was asked not to witness Lady Wallisford's departure. That wasn't to say that there weren't people hiding behind every set of curtains in that part of the house, watching with morbid curiosity.

Livinia and Cedric stood outside waiting, while Lady Pettifer was seeing Lady Wallisford down the stairs. Dory watched from Lady Pettifer's window, both needing to watch and wanting not to. She felt like she owed it to Nora to witness this.

Lady Wallisford wore a cream suit with a fur collar and a hat. She looked as if prepared for a day shopping in London, refusing to bow to circumstances. How long she would be gone from here, Dory didn't know. She deserved to be cast away from her home and family for what she had done, and she would be. Dory couldn't regret her not being hanged, as it was a brutal form of punishment in her book.

Down below, Livinia cried and Cedric looked ashen. That had to be the true punishment for Lady Wallisford, but her pride refused to let her respond, or to dent her pride. Unheard things were said and then Lady and Lord Wallisford were driven away.

There was a finality to this, the ending of something and the prevailing of justice. Dory hoped that Nora was pleased with this outcome. She seemed a sensible girl and

Dory identified with her wish to seek justice for Tilda Turman. Justice—it was an important thing.

Backing away from the window, Dory sighed. She had only been at Wallisford Hall a few weeks, but it felt much longer. In the beginning, she had been grudgingly invited, then unwanted. Helping DI Ridley had felt important; it had felt necessary and something she would not have been able to walk away from. How could someone live with themselves by not doing all they could when something happened to someone like Nora—and Tilda. These were not lives to be used up and thrown away in other people's carelessness and discard. They should certainly not be swept away for someone's ambition. Right had prevailed and Dory was pleased. A wrong had been righted and she was glad she lived in a world where that happened.

Chapter 32

ory couldn't believe she was going to France. All of a sudden, she had a path before her where she had previously felt trapped and uncertain. And they were apparently leaving very soon. Lady Pettifer wasn't wasting time, but Livinia was lamenting having to pack up so quickly.

The staff were also busy, given orders to shut down the house. Dory didn't know exactly what would happen to them, whether they would follow Lord Wallisford north for the shooting season, or perhaps some would be sent to the townhouse in Belgravia until they were needed.

There was a small sense in Dory that felt responsible for breaking this house and family apart, but she was not the one that had murdered Nora Sands. And technically, it was DI Ridley that held Lady Wallisford to account, even if he had eventually been dismissed from the case. Still, it was difficult not to feel some measure of responsibility.

Saying that, she didn't tolerate others placing blame on her. That might be hypocritical, but she didn't care.

Mavis and Clara were busy flaring white sheets across the furniture in the salon. Cedric was still in the parlor, nursing a whiskey, while Livinia expressed her unhappiness at the turn of events. Mr. Holmes attended to them while everyone else ran around and prepared for the departure.

"I guess we won't be seeing you here again," Larry said as Dory made her way out to the bench by the kitchen garden to warm herself with the sunshine and to escape the uncomfortable feeling in the house. Nothing was spoken, but she was treated like a pariah, a person everyone was wary of. Unjust, but it hurt all the same. No good deed goes unpunished, they say.

"No, I don't think so," she responded. "I am to follow Lady Pettifer."

"She seems alright."

"Yes, she is."

"Well, good luck with everything. I think you've been the shortest duration servant of this house."

"That's something to pride myself over, isn't it?"

Larry laughed. "No sign of that DI, then?"

"I understand he's been sent back to London."

"And now everyone leaves. It's right lonely here when everyone goes."

"So you have to stay?"

"Can't take the garden with them, can they?"

"No, I suppose not."

"All the flowers blooming and no one to see them."

Again, Dory felt a wave of responsibility. "You will see them."

"Best get on," Larry said. "The grass waits for no man. We're mowing today. A hell of a task." With his hands in his pockets, he wandered off, giving a quick finger salute before disappearing out of sight. Dory should be getting on as well. There was only an hour left until they left. Her things were packed, which wasn't hard when everything she had fit neatly into one small suitcase.

Predictably, Gladys was in the kitchen, topping snow peas into a bowl. She looked up when Dory walked in and sighed. "Off to greener pastures, then? France. Who would have thought?"

"Honestly, I don't know what kind of pastures they have over there. I guess I will find out."

"They won't let you travel without a passport."

"Lady Pettifer is having one arranged for me. It will be waiting for me at South Hampton."

"Say one thing for them, they do get things done quickly."

"Apparently, the secretary responsible for issuing passports is a son of one of her friends," Dory said.

"That always helps," Gladys said with a chuckle. "You be careful over there, and watch for those Frenchmen. Lie through their teeth to catch the attention of a young girl. Don't be fooled. I don't know what your mother is going to think."

"I can't stay home just because she will worry. Besides, things will get quite uncomfortable for me here when things come out. Lady Pettifer thinks it's best for everyone that I'm away for a bit."

"I suppose she is right. It's an awful business."

"At least Nora's family has some answers now."

"We all have some answers now," Gladys said with distaste. "Now don't go running off with some foreigner while you're over there. Your mother will never forgive me."

"I won't," Dory said, feeling her cheeks flare with embarrassment. "I'm not really one to run off with anyone."

"Don't think I didn't notice how you traipsed after that policeman."

"I didn't traipse," Dory said with offense. "I assisted."

"Handsome one, that one."

"Can't say I noticed," Dory said in a high voice, unable to carry the sentence with any credibility. "He's gone now and I'll likely never see him again."

"Shame."

Shame? Would she make her mind up? "I better go."

Gladys rose to give her an embrace. "You did well by Nora, even if it's unlikely I will ever be allowed to bring another family member into the house. I'll pack you a sandwich for the road."

Dory didn't know what to say. Saying goodbye was difficult enough without having to get into the whole idea of her being bothersome. Instead, she nodded and made her way out of the kitchen before she got teary.

Returning to Lady Pettifer's room, Dory completed the last of the packing. Lady Pettifer had a large trunk, four hat boxes and a case of toiletries. They would need help carrying it all down. The lady was dining with Cedric and Livinia, and they would be leaving right after. Dory went in search of George to help carry everything down and was told that all the luggage, including Livinia's sizeable trunk, would have to be driven separately, so there was nothing for Dory to do other than place her small suitcase with Lady Pettifer's luggage.

The noise downstairs told her that luncheon was finished and it was time to go.

"I'll just refresh slightly," Livinia stated and bounded up the stairs.

"We'll have a quick drink while we wait," Lady Pettifer said with a wink to Cedric, who still had the tight expression he'd had since the Commissioner had come to the house. If Dory felt responsible in some small measure for everything that had resulted, he must feel a multiple of it. He was, after all, responsible by not owning up to what he'd done, even if he held no blame for his mother's consequential actions. Dory felt sorry for him, but not as sorry as she felt for Tilda and Nora. It was all so very unfortunate.

They disappeared into the parlor, which had yet to be hidden under a blanket of sheets. After they were settled with their drinks, the staff all disappeared downstairs for their luncheon. It was the perfect time for Dory to say goodbye as they were all together.

She waited a few moments, then went downstairs. It was also the first time she'd had to confront them all after everything that had happened.

"Well, I guess I'm off," she said brightly, more so than she actually felt. It was a little frightening leaving the only country she had ever known, to land on foreign shores.

Most were staring at her dourly as if she was a viper in their midst. Mr. Holmes didn't look at her and Mrs. Parsons looked sour. "Are you eating with us?" she asked with little warmth in her voice.

"No, I am taking a sandwich with me."

Gladys got up and walked over to retrieve a paper bag for her. "Safe travels, love," she said. "And ignore them," she finished more quietly.

Clara and Mavis gave guarded waves, but wilted under Mrs. Parsons' piercing gaze.

"You know," Dory stated, her voice surprisingly strong and clear, "anyone who thinks senseless notions of propriety outweighs justice for the loss of Nora or Tilda Turman's lives have a clear defect in their character, as far as I'm concerned."

Mrs. Parsons looked away and Mr. Holmes stayed exactly like he was.

"Moral corruption," Dory stated with the righteous conviction of an offended teetotaler. It may well be the most heinous insult she could throw at Mr. Holmes and Mrs. Parsons, other than that they ran a disorderly house. They prided themselves on their standards and propriety, which apparently had no flexibility to acknowledge that their masters were absolutely in the wrong.

Turning sharply, she walked away, holding her head high, her heels clicking on the floor. Mercy, was she glad she was leaving this place with its strict insistence on conformity and convention, even at the expense of what was right. How they dealt with their own reactions was theirs to worry about. Dory was putting this all behind her and turning her thoughts to the excitement that was to come.

George was helping Lady Pettifer and Livinia into the car when Dory joined them outside. Dory had to take the little fold down seat and sit backwards for the journey. She didn't mind, but it gave her a retreating look at Wallisford Hall, where Cedric stood watching in the doorway, watching them go.

"I hate the Mediterranean in summer," Livinia said.

"I think you'll hate London even more this summer," Lady Pettifer responded and Livinia's mouth drew tight as she looked out the window.

"Will it ever blow over?"

"Maybe next year," Lady Pettifer assured her.

"Next year?" Livinia said with dismay. "What am I supposed to do in France for a whole year?"

"Maybe worry about what the Germans are up to."

"What do the Germans have to do with France?"

"Hopefully very little," Lady Pettifer said with a tightness to her smile that Dory had learnt meant she was worried.

"Papa says this war will never happen," Livinia said with absolute certainty.

"Let's hope he's right."

"Then again, if there is a war, we'll have to return to England." Livinia looked pleased with the prospect. "Mother, too."

It was Dory's turn to look out the window. How she wished Livinia wasn't coming with them. It was hard to imagine they were the same age. Every silver lining had a dark cloud, it seemed.

The End

Next book in the Dory Spark series

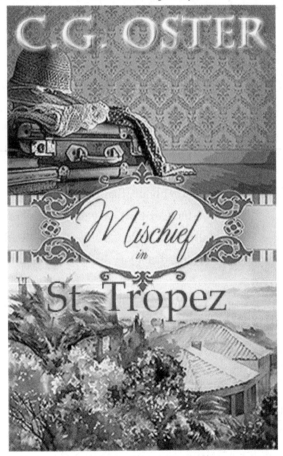

Mischief in St. Tropez – Dory Sparks Mysteries Book 2 - In the bright sunshine and glorious landscapes of the Cote D'Azur, the enclave of British high society worry about the impending war. So much so that when the body of a Hungarian noble is found at Lady Tonbridge's soiree, a haphazard investigation finds no culprit. Miss Dory Sparks, the companion to Lady Pettifer, finds herself drawn into investigating when no one else seems pay this murder its due attention.

The handsome Baron Domenik Drecsay had never been a saint and his interest in the heiresses along the coast was known by all. Miss Livinia Fellingworth had certainly been falling for his charms. Even so, Dory struggles to find a motive for his murder, and she is running out of time as the worsening situation in France threatens the decorum lives of the foreign societies along the sparkling coast.